D1645172

TIBOR DÉRY

*The Giant*

---

*Behind the Brick Wall*

---

*Love*

JOHN CALDER · LONDON

PUBLISHED IN GREAT BRITAIN 1964
BY JOHN CALDER (PUBLISHERS) LTD.
17 SACKVILLE STREET · LONDON, WI

*The Giant*, original Hungarian title *Az Óriás*, 1948
*Behind The Brick Wall*, original Hungarian title, *A Péglafal Mögött*, 1955
*Love*, original Hungarian title, *Szerelem*, 1955

PRINTED IN GREAT BRITAIN BY
BLACKIE & SON LTD., BISHOPBRIGGS, GLASGOW

# CONTENTS

# THE GIANT

*Translated by Kathleen Szasz*

# THE GIANT

A black-bearded man, wearing a thin, velvet-collared coat with split shoes through which his bare toes protruded, sat on a foot-stool with his back to the house-wall of one of the blocks of flats on Teréz Boulevard singing a Latin song. He accompanied himself on a man-sized harp which stood on the pavement in front of him on a black ebony base; its silver strings flashed in the sunlight.

> Eheu, fugaces, Postume, Postume
> Labuntur anni nec pietas moram
> Rugis et instanti senectae
> Adferet indomitaeque porti.

In a doorway close by, a woman was selling maize cakes displayed on a wooden tray, which were protected against the attacks of the flies with a thin muslin veil; a grey-haired, bespectacled man standing next to her had yeast and a pair of yellow shoes to offer to the crowd that billowed around them. Further away, in the square, the morning market was in full swing. Vendors kicked their heels in long rows before the boarded-in coffee-house windows, offering for sale second-hand suits, strudl, white bread, eider-down cases, women's worn underclothes, pocket torches, wrist-watches; a man was swinging a bunch of brand-new, black-enamelled miners' lamps on his arm, an elderly, bespectacled lady in striped men's trousers with a green turban on her head

9

was trying to barter her canary for a side of smoked bacon. The watch-peddlars were surrounded by Russian soldiers, the Russian soldiers by voluntary interpreters speaking Czech and Serbian. There were pedestrians as well walking in the middle of the road and when, at times, the Boulevard produced at one of its deserted ends a rapidly growing and then quickly shrinking lorry, the sparrows flew frightened up onto the window-sills. The street-car rails were covered in rubble from one end to the other. Andrássy Avenue was so quiet that one could clearly distinguish the thin whistle of the shunting engines from the Eastern Railway Station.

> Non, si trecennis quotquot eunt dies,
> Amice . . . .

sang the harpist turning his eyes to the sky, whose immaculate Mediterranean light painted his open-mouthed face the colour of honey.

"What language is he singing in?" asked a young girl from the back row. She was wearing pale grey men's trousers with a cherry-red tam-o'-shanter on her head.

"In Russian most likely."

"No!" a man said. "It's English."

"Do you know English?"

"Of course," the man said hitching the rucksack higher on his shoulder from which two rusty stove-pipes protruded. "Of course I know English. But I don't get this because its American."

"Holy mackerel," the young girl said with awe.

Here too it was mainly pedestrians who tramped along in the muddy road with huge rucksacks and bundles on their shoulders; some were pulling hand-carts loaded with bedding, kitchenware, furniture, sticking out their thin necks and arching their skinny backs. Most of them stopped before the harpist to rest.

"Why is he singing, I wonder . . ." the young girl said. "Nobody gives him anything."

"He sings because he is happy."

"Perhaps he wants to sell the harp," someone else ventured.

Suddenly the harpist turned his head towards them and nodded twice. A second later he shuddered, reeled over, and in slow motion collapsed with his face in the mud.

"Holy mackerel," the girl said frightened, "he must have fainted!"

They turned the lifeless body on its back, someone knelt down by it and felt for the heart. "He won't sing English no more," the man said rising, beat the mud from his knee and walked on. A sudden concourse stood for a while round the body, then scattered. Most of them lined up before the vendor in the near-by doorway and viewed the displayed yellow shoes. A long-legged fair-haired lad picked up the harp from beside the body, tilted it on his shoulder and set out, groaning, towards Andrássy Avenue.

"Where are you taking that thing?" someone asked.

"For a walk," the lad groaned. "Why? Do you want it?"

"Not me."

"Because you can have it," the lad grumbled, "why shouldn't you get crippled?" He pushed the instrument further back on his shoulder and at the sudden movement every string of the harp broke into ringing tones. The sunshine ran sparkling over the silver net.

A group of women marched along the road with picks and

shovels thrown over their shoulders. The red-capped girl turned round and her lively black eyes which blazed as if spring itself had set them on fire, studied the slack-shouldered, listlessly shuffling women. She counted them to see whether there weren't thirteen, then suddenly she spun round as though aware in her bones that someone was staring at her.

"You! What are you staring at?" she asked sinking both hands in her trouser pockets and pushing out her chest with boyish impudence; her two tiny breasts almost pierced through the red flannel blouse. "Do I have a hole in my pants?"

Her mocking eyes measured the stranger from head to foot, then she fished a sunflower seed from her pocket, bit it in two with her tiny white teeth, spat out the husk, and from the corner of her eye gave the stranger another look. Then, unexpectedly, she blushed and lowered her eyes.

The man was so tall that, had she wanted to kiss him, she would have had to climb on to a foot-stool. A lock of his flaxen-coloured hair had fallen over his forehead; again and again the April wind swept it aside but it was so thick and heavy that it slid immediately back into place, in the middle of the domed, freckled forehead, between the two protruding brow-ridges that held together the huge, round face like a hoop. The snub nose in the centre of the big face had come out somewhat smaller than planned; it was the only witty detail amidst the huge forms hewn out with a hatchet, whose rawness not even the resigned, mild blue eyes could relieve. His hands were as oversized as selfishness in the human soul and his feet in the size 52 shoes could have been the symbol of a nation getting back on its feet.

"Golly! The Lord sure ladled you out with a big spoon!"

the girl said alarmed and quickly pulled her hands from her pockets. "What did your good mother have to say when she first laid eyes on you?"

The big hunk of man blushed and gazed in mute amazement at the girl from his mild blue eyes. She shook her head in annoyance.

"What is your name?" she asked severely. "Look, why don't you introduce yourself to a lady if you want to talk to her?"

"But I didn't want to talk to you," the man said surprised.

The girl stamped her feet.

"Fiddlesticks!" she said, "of course you did. What's your name?"

"István Kovács Jr.," the giant replied blushing anew.

"Nice name," the girl opined giving the man a long, dreamy look from her shining black eyes. "A real nice name. Mine is Juli. Juli Szandál. Say 'glad to meet you'!"

"I beg your pardon?" the man said.

"Say 'glad to meet you'," the girl cried banging her two tiny fists together in her anger. "See here, has no one ever taught you how to introduce yourself to a lady? And why didn't you ask your mother to patch up your trousers before you went out? There's a hole in them big enough for me to stick my head through!"

István Kovács Jr. looked down at his trousers, then carefully covered the hole with his palm.

"That's better," Juli said approvingly, "much more elegant! Are you going to walk like that now, with your hand on your knee? . . . Tell me, why are you crying?"

The man turned away his face without answering.

"Why are you crying?" the girl repeated curiously.

"I always do when someone mentions my mother," the man replied wiping away his tears with the back of his hand. "You couldn't call it crying, it's only that my eyes fill with tears."

"Is your mother dead?"

István Kovács Jr. nodded.

"Interesting," the girl said, "so is mine. And your father?"

"He's gone long ago . . ."

"Then we are in the same boat," the girl cried, "because mine is also dead, though he hasn't been dead long, only three months, during the siege. Now you see," she added contentedly, "we are both little orphans."

She looked up at István Kovács Jr. and started laughing: that "little orphan" was so big that he could have made a whole orphanage sit on his knee. A lovely hunk of man, the girl thought, but a bit barmy. With a gay little movement she pushed the red beret back on her head and laughed again into the man's face. He stood looking back at her with a solemn, motionless face, resting his chin on his breast. But the girl's sweet laughter so tickled his ears, its irresistible waves so swayed his heart, that his shiny snub-nose quivered, his brows lifted, his eyes narrowed, his lips stretched: he burst out laughing.

"What are you grinning at, Cheshire cat?" Juli asked severely.

"Hahaha," István Kovács Jr. laughed, "hahaha!"

"I've never seen a cart-horse laugh," the girl said, "but I bet it looks like you when it does."

"Hahaha," István Kovács Jr. laughed, "hahaha!"

Now Juli had to join in too because she had never seen any-

one laugh with his entire body the way this barmy giant did.
He laughed and winked at her with his eyes and slapped his
thighs resoundingly. When Juli stopped for a second because
she was out of breath, all she had to do was glance at Kovács
Jr.'s torn pink shirt, which, impelled by his shaking belly had
suddenly slipped from his trousers and was now dancing like
a small apron over his stomach, and off she was again in new
peals of laughter. "For heaven's sake stop, Cheshire cat!" she
panted, pressing one hand to her stomach and wiping her eyes
with the other, "you'll kill me, you fascist!"

"Hahaha, fascist!" Kovács Jr. thundered, "hahaha!"

Someone stopped behind their backs, then walked on.
"Shame," his voice floated behind him, "laughing like that
beside a dead body!"

The two fell suddenly silent and looked at each other.
Abruptly the street lay open before them—like a waking dream
—and in a second it had sucked them into its common stream.
A new group of rubble-clearing women marched by with
picks and shovels on their shoulders . . . or were they the same
women? Right along the street, as far as the eye could see,
fragments and slivers of glass flashed their luminous eyes in the
layer of mud and debris that covered the side-walk as they
blinked at the sun.

"Lord!" Juli exclaimed delighted, "this whole street is looking back at the sky! Beautiful! . . . Why don't you push back
your shirt?" she grumbled, looking querulously at Kovács Jr.
who was staring into her face, his ponderous head thrown
back, his mouth open, smiling happily. "One should pull this
dead daddy into a doorway!"

"Shall I carry him in?" the giant asked quietly and, stretching his neck forward examined the body.

Juli shrugged her shoulders.

"If your two doll's arms can take it," she said mockingly, "but don't you dare moan!"

"If I can take it?" Kovács Jr. wagged his head disapprovingly, "I don't know what you mean, Miss. I can lift a small man like this with one arm."

"Truly?"

The giant blushed.

"What do you mean truly?"

"I don't believe it," Juli said. "Not with one arm."

Kovács Jr. was so ashamed now that even his neck turned dark red. He hung his head and looked down on the ground which was, apparently, unwilling to open before him. "Well?" said the girl suddenly losing patience.

"Listen to me, Miss Juli," said István Kovács Jr. in a shaky voice, "I always speak the truth. I once lifted a medium-sized cow with one arm."

Juli shook her head.

"You can't lead me up the garden path," she informed him. "The dead are very heavy, I know it, because I was alone when my father died and I couldn't move him though I am not a weakling either."

Without a word István Kovács Jr. turned away, went over to the body lying along the house wall and went down on one knee beside it. Carefully he raised the dead body to a sitting position, resting its back against his chest so it shouldn't keel over, then he reached one arm under the man's knees, held him close as if he were holding an infant in his arm, then, with a single tensing of his powerful thigh muscles he rose. Not even his neck turned red.

"Whew!" sounded a voice behind him. From the sudden

jerk the dead man's black-bearded head fell forward and one of his limp arms began to swing.

By the time István Kovács Jr. returned from under the door-way the girl in the red beret had disappeared. He waited for a while, anxiously studying the passers-by and searching the audience assembling around the vendors, then, thrusting both fists into his trouser pockets he set off. He had almost reached the Western Railway Station when someone pinched his arm from behind with sharp, pointed nails.

"So it's no use my hiding from you, you Cheshire cat," Juli panted indignantly, her face pink with running, "you aren't even trying to find me! I almost lost you, you silly orphan!"

Kovács Jr. stopped in his tracks, stared at the girl and brought together his two huge palms thunderously. Several passers-by turned back and watched the surprised giant with a gay smile.

"You were hiding, Miss Juli?" he murmured amazed, "and you wanted me to find you?"

His face with its perplexed snub nose and the half-open mouth was the very image of happy wonder; worry had not ploughed a single furrow, nor had experience brushed with its incendiary breath the large, playful, childishly smooth plains of his face, which offered themselves pink and bestrewn with golden fluff to the Furies. The infantile smoothness of the complexion was marred only by two blemishes: a nail-sized brown wart trembling on the top of the left brow and the almost invisible flaxen-coloured hairs curling under the chin that also reminded one of the foetal scalp-hair of a new-born baby. His gums were also healthily pink like an infant's, his teeth marched straight and milky white towards the gullet and his lips were full and cherry-red.

"You wanted me to look for you, Miss Juli?" he repeated open-mouthed, clapping his two palms again in wonder.

"The hell I did!" Juli said angrily.

The giant took the girl's hand and drew her down beside him on the steps of the railway station. Behind them, a few steps higher up, an old woman was sunning herself, her eyes shut and not far away a bespectacled gentleman of school-masterish appearance was offering matches, flints and a flowery, gold-coloured eider-down case to the passers-by.

"You are not afraid of me, Miss Juli, are you?" asked Kovács Jr. and stared into the girl's face, his mouth open again with excitement and curiosity. "Everybody is afraid of me, Miss Juli. Tell me now, is it my fault that I look so awful? And yet I never swear, I never pick a quarrel, I never take a dirty word in my mouth . . . Or are you afraid too?" he asked fearfully after a while when he noticed that the girl was grimacing.

"I am frightened too," Juli said.

The giant rose.

"Then I am going, Miss Juli," he said sadly.

"Wait!" Juli cried. "Sit down again. If you can prove to me that I have nothing to fear from you then I won't be frightened."

Kovács Jr. stared ahead of him morosely.

"How can I prove that?" he asked frowning.

"I'll tell you," Juli said. "If you hold out your cheek and let me slap you with all my force for the whole street to see, and if you give me your word of honour that you'll do nothing to me, I'll believe you."

The man shook his head in disbelief.

"And then you won't be afraid?" he asked.

"Then I won't," said the girl.

Kovács Jr. thought it over.

"You won't be afraid of me then?" he asked after a little while. "Never again," Juli promised.

"My father's name was Milan Kovachich," the giant said quietly, "he was the strongest man in the village. He was a good two head taller than me and he hanged himself, because of a woman, on an elm in front of the council house so everyone should see him in the morning. That's when I came to Budapest."

"Kovachich?" the girl said, "you are spinning a yarn. There is no such name."

The man blushed.

"My father was a Serb," he said, "and my mother Austrian. The first branch broke under his weight but the second held good. No woman has touched me since, Miss Juli. And now hit me if you want to."

The girl's eyes flashed: the giant brought his face slowly closer.

"And you really won't hurt me?" she asked and her voice became furry with excitement.

The man shook his head silently.

"Cross your heart?"

"Yes," the man said. "I give you my word of honour."

The girl swallowed convulsively, her throat was suddenly dry.

"It isn't true," she said, "you'll beat me to death if I do it. You'll squash me like a bug. I daren't do it."

"Do it!" the giant whispered and closed his eyes.

Juli bit her lips and her toes curled in with excitement. For a second she hesitated, then with a deep sigh she slowly lifted her hand and with outstretched arm she slapped the man with all her strength. At the sharp crack the old woman sitting behind them opened her eyes and several people turned back. A round, purple patch appeared on the man's cheek.

"Did it hurt?" Juli asked from behind clenched teeth. Her eyes closed for a moment. "Did it hurt?"

The man still hadn't withdrawn his face.

"No," he said in a low voice looking into the girl's dulled eyes. Suddenly she lifted her arms, flung them around the giant's neck and kissed him on the lips. The next moment she jumped up and with an involuntary, modest movement—as if she were smoothing down her skirt—she drew her hand down her side.

"We can go now," she whispered.

Juli lived in one of the cellar compartments of a József Borough air-raid shelter, and there they went first. There wasn't much to pack, everything Fate had preserved of Juli's wealth fitted easily into a tiny knotted string shopping-bag. From the József Borough it was a long walk to the outer Angyalföld, V. Street, where Kovács Jr. nested in the deserted office building of a lumber yard; towards the end of the journey Juli began to limp. To cheer her up, Kovács Jr. broke into a song.

"What are you muttering, Cheshire Cat?" the girl asked.

The giant raised his voice a little.

> Eheu fugaces, Postume, Postume,
> Labuntur anni nec pietas moram.

"Bless my soul!" Juli exclaimed, "if it isn't the English song that musician sang! Do you know it too?"

"No, I don't know it," the man said, "but I have funny ears. When I really listen to something I only have to hear it once. Not to my dying day will I forget a single one of the words you say to me in this life, Miss Juli."

Juli blushed.

"I am not falling for this," she said and stopped. "I don't believe a word you say. Tell me what I first said to you, Cheshire Cat!"

The giant bowed his head, his forehead drew into deep wrinkles.

"You, what are you staring at? Do I have a hole in my pants?"

Juli clapped her hands.

"Did I really say that? And then?"

"Golly! The Lord sure ladled you out with a big spoon!" Kovács Jr. continued. "What did your good mother have to say when she first laid eyes on you? What is your name? Why don't you introduce yourself to a lady if you want to talk to her?"

Juli turned pale.

"Did I really say that?"

Kovács Jr.'s forehead was covered in big drops of perspiration.

"My name is Juli. Juli Szandál. Say 'glad to meet you'. Why didn't you ask your mother to patch up your trousers before you went out? There's a hole in them big enough for me to stick my head through. Why are you crying? Is your mother dead?"

"You did cry, you know . . ." Juli said. "You are a queer one, you are, Cheshire Cat. Now what are you stopping for?"

They stood before the wooden gate of a tall fence. Kovács Jr. raised his head.

"We have arrived," he said tiredly. "Shall I go on? 'We are both little orphans.'"

"That's true," Juli said, "but if you don't open this triumphal arch this very minute I am turning back right now . . . Why don't you carry me in your arms?"

The girl stood motionless in the dense summer moonlight and sang. Her two luminous white arms arched upwards and then, breaking at an angle, slanted back towards her nape; she threw the slender shadow of a Greek vase upon the moonlit road. The vase was filled with happiness and melody.

Behind her in the lumber-yard the tall stacks of boards at times crackled in the light and relayed their dry cracking sound back into the night as the voice of silence. The path before the narrow, low office building was covered in a thick layer of sawdust that swallowed up every sound but, like a sheet laid out to dry, reflected and scattered the silver moonlight in the darkness. The girl stood in her bare feet in the centre of the sheet with the Greek shadow behind her back, her face turned towards the office building; the two moonlit windows, trembling in the breeze, cut flashing into the suburban landscape. Here the moonlight was so soft and thick that it seemed, in places, to be a strange, new summer vegetation that had suddenly overrun the narrow little streets between the wooden fences, climbed up the white, hairy boards and spread with lightning speed to flood in a moment the entire lumber yard. Here and there, under a protruding roof-edge or a thick-crowned tree the delicate vegetation encircled a slice of unsullied, dark-blue shade; but it retreated, quivering, when the breeze rocked the rustling crown of the tree. No sound penetrated from the street; only from the far side, at the distant corner of the yard, did the low lapping of the Danube waves merge with the silence.

Juli finished her song.

"Are you asleep?" she called in a low voice into the moonlight behind her.

There was no answer. For a while she listened, laughing up with her flashing white teeth at the full moon that stood motionless above her head, then she shivered and with a stretching, lazy motion untied her two light-besprinkled, hard little hands from behind her head.

"Are you asleep?" she repeated. Again she received no answer. "Of course you aren't asleep," she continued quietly, "because if you were you would snore and you aren't snoring. But if you aren't asleep why don't you answer me, Cheshire Cat?"

István Kovács Jr. was lying on top of a tall pyre of boards behind her back, looking up at the moon with parted lips. About his round massive head the flaxen-coloured waves of hair sparkled in the light.

"I'm not asleep," he said.

The girl shrugged her shoulders.

"I knew that anyway, Cheshire Cat," she hummed; "well then, what are you doing?"

"Nothing," Kovács Jr. replied and his heart swelled with happiness until it almost exploded his barrel chest.

"If you aren't doing anything, let's play," Juli suggested.

"Let's," Kovács Jr. agreed.

The girl turned, ran on tip-toe to the stack and lithely, like a cat, climbed in a second to the top. For a while the disturbed moonlight whirled excitedly about her, then, appeased, it settled down again on her tiny ears, her slender neck and her gleaming thighs from which the wind had swept up the light little skirt.

"I love you, Cheshire Cat," said Juli, then squatted down quickly and with the point of her index finger drew a light circle on Kovács Jr.'s red-checked shirt above his heart. "And you?"

Kovács Jr.'s eyes filled with tears.

"When did you first say that you loved me?" Juli asked, drawing a big interrogation mark in the middle of the circle. "Is it a month yet?"

"One month."

Juli drew a figure 1 next to the interrogation mark.

"Why so late?"

"Just because . . ." murmured Kovács Jr.

"You didn't have the courage to tell me?"

Kovács Jr. signalled with his head that he didn't.

"Yet, how many days have we known each other?"

"Fifty-nine," said Kovács Jr.

"And how many days since you loved me?"

"Fifty-nine," said Kovács Jr.

Juli put her palm on the man's mouth.

"It isn't true," she said quickly, "it isn't fifty-nine days. You've loved me for ever and ever. And what did I say when you asked me if I loved you?"

"You told me to go and see my grandmother in Graz," Kovács Jr. said happily.

"Shame on me," cried Juli, "it isn't true, I love you too! . . . And what else did I say?"

"You said if I loved you I should buy you a pair of shoes."

"It is still not too late for that," Juli informed him, carefully examining her small, muscular foot, its shy toes hidden to their roots in the sparkling sawdust. The wind was driving a quick summer cloud across the sky above their heads: the brilliance congealed suddenly and darkness descended on the yard. The moon's ephemeral yellow vegetation turned black in a second and fell off the fence and the house opposite; it survived only in the distant corner of the yard and, as if it wanted to flee to Buda, ran across the water of the Danube that rocked it ecstatically on minute waves.

"Oh, it's gone dark!" Juli cried; but already one of her toes began to shine again. A thick beam of light broke through a crevice in the cloud, bathing the two figures on top of the stack in its precipitous luminosity.

"And what did I say when I ran away from you on the third day?" Juli asked.

"Nothing," Kovács Jr. replied morosely.

"And what did I say when I returned two days later?"

"You quarrelled with me."

"But what did I say?"

"A lot."

"Repeat word for word what I said," she cried discontentedly. "What was the first sentence? I'll squash your up-turned little nose!"

István Kovács Jr. covered the girl's tiny fist with his palm.

"If you keep on tickling my nose I can't talk," he informed her. "Take your hand off me! You said," he continued and his voice turned suddenly heavy, "don't think for a moment that I am sorry. I came back because I have nowhere to sleep. What are you grinning for? I am going!"

"And then?" the girl asked.

"Then you ate."

"But what else did I say?"

"You ate a lot," Kovács Jr. said thoughtfully.

The girl replaced her fist on his nose.

"I'll squash it!" she threatened. "What did I say?"

"You said," István Kovács Jr. replied, "you said while you were eating: 'hmmm . . . he . . . ccc . . . ehem . . . so!' and then: 'Is that all?'"

"Here, I'll squash it!" the girl announced.

"You said," Kovács Jr. continued, "Is that all? Then let me tell you that I came back only because I haven't eaten for two days. And now I am going. But let me warn you first: next time you bring a woman out here . . ."

The man fell silent and his huge, round face, silver in the moonlight, distorted with pain.

"Go on," the girl said.

"Next time you bring a woman out here," Kovács Jr. continued, sinking his head in his hands while his forehead broke out in perspiration, "next time you bring a woman out here, make sure who she is before sharing your last pot of soup with her, do you get me, brother in misery? And now I'm going."

"Heavens, did I really say that?" Juli asked. "Word for word? But I didn't go, did I? I never meant to go . . . It never even occurred to me!"

"Is that true?" Kovács Jr. asked unbelieving and with an unexpected, quick motion he sat up. The thick boards below him emitted a sharp squeak. His huge face—tossed hither and thither between pain and happiness—reflected deep amazement. "Is it true you didn't want to go? Then why did you run away?"

"Hush, brother in misery," Juli whispered, shutting the man's mouth. "Let's not talk about that. I ran away because . . ."

She fell silent and for a moment her heart was again filled with the old anxiety. The man's improbably smooth face with the expectantly opened mouth and the wondering, innocent eyes was so close to her face that his breath brushed her eyes. Suddenly the girl raised her hand and slapped him with all her might.

"Because I was afraid of you," she said hoarsely. "That is why I ran away . . ."

Both were silent. Another cloud slid beneath the moon, the Pest shore darkened again, only the distant Buda mountains retained their hazy brilliance. With a childish gesture Kovács Jr. pressed his palm to his burning cheek.

"When I let you slap me at the Western Railway Station," he said sadly, "you promised that you would never be afraid of me again. True?"

"True," Juli said rising. "Come to bed."

"Are you still afraid?" Kovács Jr. asked in a shaky voice.

"No," Juli said. "Or rather, yes. Because one day you'll have your revenge on me."

"My revenge?" the man asked dumbfounded. "For what?"

"I don't know," the girl said. "For everything. Come now!"

They slept in the back room of the office building on a straw-sack laid on the floor topped at the head with three folded wheat-sacks. Window and door remained open so that they should hear if anyone tried to climb the fence into the lumber yard. They could not rely on the age-stopped ears of Uncle Fecske, the other guard, who slept at the other end of the yard. When it was very warm Juli would toss about in her sleep and belabour Kovács Jr.'s big naked body with her purposeful fists until, grumbling, he slid from the straw-sack on to the floor, resting his head on his arm. István Kovács Jr. slept lightly, the first twittering of the sparrows at dawn woke him. He woke happy as a child and leaving the husk of sleep on the floor he threw himself in a second into his clothes and the joys of the day.

"Where are you going, Cheshire Cat?" Juli asked, still dozing and turned over.

István Kovács Jr. gazed at the girl's tiny bared breast and felt like singing.

"Where are you going?" Juli repeated, slipping one round knee from under the heavy horse-blanket that lay like a board on her frilly dream.

"What did you say? . . . Public works? . . . But you've been three times already this week . . ."

"Three times?" Kovács Jr. repeated amazed. "Impossible!"

"Not only possible . . . certain . . ." Juli murmured.

"They always tell me to come," the giant said apologetically. "I'm going to ask them why!"

But Juli was asleep again.

"Sweet Cheshire Cat . . ." she whispered in a faint voice, "barmy Cheshire Cat! Why?"

The sun shone with the same full and perfect light as the moon had the night before, only the smell of the lumber yard had changed from night smell to day smell: the dry and slightly acid perfume of the oak and beech planks crackling in the sun stood like a pillar above the yard, seeping heavily into the smallest crevice and enwrapping every movement. By the time Uncle Fecske knocked at the door of the office building around half past eight the whole yard was ringing with radiance.

"Has he gone to work again?" the old man grumbled, pulling at his empty pipe and throwing a bad-tempered glance at the girl crouching on the window-sill.

"Yeah," she said swinging her bare legs gaily.

The old man cupped his hand against his ear.

"I can't hear you," he growled. "What did you say?"

"I said: yeah!" Juli cried. "Take off your shirt, Uncle Fecske!"

"What for?"

"Laundry day!" the girl shouted at the top of her voice. "I am washing the Cheshire Cat's second shirt. Off with it, Uncle Fecske, one . . . two!"

The old man shook his head. "It ain't necessary," he said. "What's the use of washing it so often. It'll only wear out. You washed it last time."

"That was in April," Juli agreed. "Go on, Uncle Fecske, no bargaining or I'll tear it off you!"

"What did you say?" the old man asked backing towards the door. "It doesn't need all that washing. Besides, where do you get the soap?"

"If you don't take it off you get no dinner," Juli informed him quietly. Strangely enough the old man heard her immediately. "What's there for dinner?" he asked pulling the shirt over his head. But his pipe that he didn't bother to take out of his mouth got stuck in a tear in the shirt, protruded through the hole and stopped the manœuvre.

"What happened?" the old man asked in a dull voice from inside the shirt, his arms raised to the sky. "Why doesn't this rag come off? Are you holding it down, Miss Juli?"

"Yes," Juli replied from the window-sill.

"I can't hear you," the old man grumbled within the shirt. "Let it go or you'll tear it. You hear me? I'll rap your fingers!"

Behind him the door opened: a lanky, skinny ancient fellow with a grey beard stood on the threshold. For a while he meditatively observed the headless phenomenon standing in the middle of the room and waving desperate arms towards the sky, then he slowly raised his stick and pointed to it.

"And what may this be?" he asked in his improbably deep voice which sounded as if a whole network of tunnels had rolled it out.

"That's Uncle Fecske," said Juli.

"And where is his head?" greybeard asked amazed, "won't he fall over without a head?"

The pipe clattered on the ground and the next second Uncle Fecske emerged red as a crab from the filthy waves of his shirt.

"I asked you what is for dinner," he grumbled, gnashing his yellow teeth. "What makes you show up here so early in the morning, Csipesz?"

The lanky old man backed away frightened.

"Stay, Uncle Csipesz," Juli exclaimed. "You'd better take off your shirt too, and be quick about it."

"Does she want to give us a beating?" the ancient fellow asked, his yellow fingers playing a tattoo on his beard. "Please, don't hit me, I haven't stolen anything from you, little Miss!"

By the time Kovács Jr. returned an hour later the three shirts were drying in the sun in front of the office building. The old men sat on the ground bare to the waist, their backs against the sun-warmed wall, measuring each other silently and wryly.

"Are you through already, Cheshire Cat?" Juli cried from the window. Tell me, what's in that big parcel you brought?"

"Bread and potatoes," replied Kovács Jr., standing, his feet apart, his face raised to the sky, the very statue of happiness, over old age crouching on the ground. "I got it from the Russians."

"And how come they let you come home so early?"

"I don't know," Kovács Jr. replied. "They said I'd worked enough this week, I could go home, *davaj*! What are you doing, Uncles?"

Old Csipesz picked himself up groaning from the ground, stepped up to the giant, raised himself on tip-toe, kissed him right and left, then sat back again.

"He wants a free dinner, the scoundrel," grumbled Uncle Fecske, giving the ancient fellow raking through his beard a disgusted look. "He isn't as half-witted as he pretends to be . . . Have you been to the main office, Mr. Kovács?"

"What for?" the giant asked amazed.

Strangely enough Uncle Fecske always understood him however quietly he spoke. "What for?" he repeated blinking nervously. "For the weekly wages, Mr. Kovács! Or do you want me to limp in for them to the other end of town on my bad feet? You could have got the money two days ago. By now it isn't worth half as much!"

"Scatterbrain, you forgot again!" Juli cried, "and yet I whispered it in your ear specially this morning."

István Kovács Jr. forgot everything nowadays—except Juli. Now again, as he set out once more towards town to fetch

the weekly wages he had to turn back at the gate because he
had forgotten to tell her that the Russians had given him meat
as well and that he had invited ten people for dinner. He was
already at the Western Railway Station but his eyes and his
ear-drums were still busy with the unforgettable moment—
adhering to the indestructible series of old memories like new
limestone rings in a stalactite—that ordinary but unique and
never to be recaptured moment when the girl laughed at him.
You got meat, she asked clapping her hands and laughing at
him. You got meat, she asked again and again along Váczi
Street, she clapped her hands and laughed and laughed. In
front of the Western Railway Station there was no other
sound but the smack of the two girlish palms.

Love wants reiteration of every fleeting moment. As it
slowly fulfils itself, so its essence—man holding out his arms
yearningly—receives less nourishment from the future and
turns more and more towards the past. All that had once been
promised by hope and imagination, all that the beloved, like
a generous goddess, had ever redeemed could be recaptured
in a moment. There is one thing only that he can no longer
reach with his hands outstretched in yearning: the fleeting
past. Exact and blissful experience has ousted all dreams from
his heart. Imagination can no longer replace the tangible
components of happiness but rejects the future and turns to
the past. Fulfilled love reaches out. The first unforgettable
kiss must be relived, the second, the third, the sweetness of the
first meeting, the first fear and pain. The past must renew
itself in its magical and unfathomable fulfilment. Kovács Jr.
did not even try to imagine how the girl would laugh at him
in the afternoon when he returned home from the main office,
but the memory of her laughter an hour earlier when he put

down the meat on the window-sill in front of her continued to vibrate in him with the alluring authenticity of reality and he yearned for it so hard that it almost broke his heart. Teréz Boulevard and Aradic Street resounded in all their length with happy, girlish laughter. But István Kovács Jr. heard that laughter only because he yearned for it, and he yearned for it because he was afraid of not hearing it any longer.

"Good, we are having a party!" Juli cried and, leaning out of the window, she threw both arms round Kovács Jr.'s neck and pressed her face, flushed with excitement, to his. In the cool of obscurity of the Aradi Street doorway the two white arms stretched out again, multiplied and reaching out from oblivion on every stair, embraced the rememberer's shoulders that stooped more and more in the twofold fever of burial and creation.

"Glory! It'll be exactly like a wedding feast," Juli cried, "and on our sixtieth day too!"

Kovács Jr. straightened up and, his back stiff, carried the wedding feast up to the second floor. He stopped at the office door and with his palm wiped Juli's burning face from his.

"Do get us a little oil and at least three onions, darling muddlehead," he heard her cry from the staircase and he pulled the door shut behind him. Two clerks were sitting in the office at the desk and two gentlemen were talking at the window. He had to wait half an hour.

"Listen, Kovács, let me warn you once more, don't allow any stranger into the yard!" the director said. "If you prove worthy of my confidence now . . ."

István Kovács Jr.'s strange memory retained—with frightening exactitude—only what he paid close attention to and he could pay close—childishly devoted—attention only to what touched his heart. Even before he walked out of the door he had already forgotten what would happen if he "proved worthy of the director's confidence". He was so absent-minded that he forgot to say good-bye to the director and so sharp-eyed, that he immediately noticed Juli with her happy and surprised face in the staircase.

"You got meat?" the girl asked, clapping her hands and laughing up to him.

István Kovács Jr. stumbled heavily down the stairs with the terrific weight of sixty days on his shoulders; those coming towards him gave way startled, then stopped to look after him. He seemed strong enough to knock a bull down and was so weak that a memory was to knock him out.

It was afternoon when he got back, Juli was waiting for him at the gate.

"Thank God you are here!" she cried from afar. "Did you bring the oil? What's the matter? You are crying?"

The giant gazed at the girl motionless, a thick layer of per-spiration stood out on his forehead and his two vertically hanging white-fluffed hands shook. His long, flaxen-coloured hair descended towards his shoulders like a sparkling silver cascade. Juli took an involuntary step backwards.

"Why aren't you laughing?" Kovács Jr. asked.

"Are you out of your mind?" Juli shouted. "Why should I laugh when I am so excited about the party. Did you bring oil?"

Kovács Jr. made no reply. Once more he searched the girl's face, with such deadly curiosity and alarm as if she had just risen from the dead, then he bent forward, encircled her with one arm and threw the immediately acquiescent, relaxed body over his shoulder. He gave a loud yell and began to run

with her towards the office building. The two old men in
their freshly laundered shirts who were sitting before the door
flew apart startled.

"What are you scared of, Uncles?" Kovács Jr. bellowed in
his thunderous voice. "Hahaha, take care not to wet your
trousers, Uncles, hahaha! Sit down again!"

In the meantime, Juli had regained her composure on
Kovács Jr.'s shoulder and began to belabour him with her two
bare feet and knees and tear the man's long fair hair so desperately with her two wild hands, that he let her gently down
on the ground.

"Where is the oil? How much was it?" she panted.

"I don't know," Kovács Jr. replied. "Hahaha . . . Uncles!"

"A pint . . ." Juli measured the bottle with her eyes.
"How much have you left?"

"Nothing," the man said shaking his head. "It cost exactly
as much as they gave me at the office."

Silence fell. Juli held up the bottle of oil to the sun.

"The whole trade should be gassed!" she said. "Then
you didn't buy onions at all."

István Kovács Jr. dropped his head on his chest and his face
turned slowly pale.

"But I did," he said after a while and his brows slid up
suddenly to the edge of his forehead. "I bought three, there
was enough money left."

"Well, hand them over."

"I can't," Kovács Jr. said.

"What do you mean you can't?" the girl asked wonderingly. "Why can't you?"

"Because I ate them," the man murmured, hanging his
his head.

Uncle Csipesz who was standing at the door holding on with both hands to his long grey beard stepped forward and put his right arm about the giant's shoulder.

"Without bread?" he asked curiously.

It was still light when, towards seven o'clock, the guests began to arrive. The veal goulash simmered in a huge cauldron under the sky in front of the office building and the unaccustomed smell had attracted a row of sparrows to the eaves, while the homeless dogs of the neighbourhood assembled in a pack outside in the street and, churning up the dust along the tall fence listened to the crackling of the fire, their tails between their legs, their mouths watering, their eyes blood-suffused. When darkness fell a few bats appeared from among the ruins of a near-by mill flapping their heavy wings in the summer night.

It was Uncle Fecske who had acquired five onions, red pepper and salt from the inn-keeper in M. Street who then arrived for dinner with his wife and ten-year-old son, and several of the guests donated bread and wine. Each guest came equipped with a plate, a knife and fork and as much good cheer and appetite as found room in their wasted bodies and souls. The meat was still half raw when all of them were already there around the cauldron.

"How many are there of us?" asked an anxious female voice.

"Fourteen . . . fifteen . . . sixteen . . . eighteen!"

"Our host included?" inquired another guest, a tall, red-headed woman holding a black cat on her lap.

"Twice over," the former female voice replied. "I hear that he goes berserk when he isn't properly fed."

"And then I suppose he'll chase the whole company out of

here?" the red-headed woman asked laughing as if tickled.
"With a veal-bone in his hand like Samson chasing the
Philistines. But what did he ask so many people for?"

"When was it we saw meat last, my son?" a clean-faced
old woman with a grey bun asked her son who, caressing his
bristly chin stared soundlessly at the steaming cauldron with
big, buck-teeth and protruding eyes. A thin rivulet of saliva
ran from the corner of his mouth.

"How should I know?" he murmured, turning livid.
"Six months . . . a year!"

"The last time I ate meat," a barefooted lad sitting next to
him wearing a camouflage patterned pair of army trousers
tied round his waist with a thick rope informed him, "on the
day my mother washed my feet during the siege . . . It was
horse meat," he added swallowing, "she brought it in from
the street . . ."

"And you haven't washed your feet since, have you son?"
the old woman asked.

"What's that to you?" the lad grimaced. "I've no shoes to
take off, have I?"

A snub-nosed, freckled girl who, tickled by the sharp
claws of hunger, was constantly giggling, broke into loud
laughter; during the entire evening her pointed giggle penetrated into all the crevices of the conversation filling them with
its thin, nervous matter.

"Tonight, after dinner you'll wash them, won't you?"

The excitement thickened quietly; some held it in silence,
but in most cases it settled under people's tongues and made
them wag. It was a stifling evening, and the heat as well lay
heavy on the guests' nerves.

Uncle Csipesz, his beard bristling, circled the fire unceasingly, with rocking shoulders, like a bear in a cage, enclosed in the cauldron's smell of meat; a young locksmith with a stooping back whom nobody knew and who opened his mouth but once in the course of the evening, licked his palms with excitement. Juli stood beside the fire stirring the slowly cooking meat with a long splinter of wood; the glare of the fire painted her unconsciously smiling little face the colour of dusk and it was lit up from inside by the double current of pride in giving and housewifely modesty. Her lips parted, her pink tongue glittered excitedly between her tiny white teeth. In honour of the guests she had put on her beautiful red flannel blouse; the perspiration never stopped running down her back and tickling her so that she, too, had to laugh. "Has no one got a pinch of salt?" she cried desperately. "Oh dear, no one will eat this, it's so tasteless!"

Behind her a young man with a clipped moustache, smooth hair and a carefully shaved face rose from a pile of boards and stepped close to her. The improvised spoon in Juli's hand knocked against the cauldron.

"What did you say, Bellus?" she called loudly over her shoulder. "That you can help me? Well?"

"In several ways, at that."

"Well, for heaven's sake, let's hear them!" the girl laughed impatiently.

"How about two handfuls of salt, if . . ." the man whispered in her ear.

Juli turned back immediately.

"Fine, hand it over!" she cried. "Where do you keep it, in your trouser pocket?"

The man laughed.

"There."

"Damn you, man, why don't you give it here, you brute, what are you waiting for?"

The man bent still closer and whispered something in her ear.

"What? . . . I'm on my way!" the girl replied in a changed voice and walked away from him slowly. "Just ring when you are ready!" Suddenly she stopped and faced him. "Do you or don't you give me that salt?"

The young man stroked his moustache.

"You heard me."

"Repeat it!" Juli's voice rang with so much irritation that several people turned towards her. "Repeat it No . . . not in a whisper! Out loud. Where shall I go tonight?"

Some of the people sitting behind them had fallen silent. Uncle Csipesz who, in his prowling, had reached the area behind Juli stopped in his tracks and, holding on to his beard bent curiously forward. "Where do you have to go, Miss Juli?" he inquired in his deep bass voice. "Do you have to go now?" From the other side of the circle the voracious giggle of the snub-nosed, freckled girl came streaming towards them and flowed around the sudden silence.

"Shame on you!" Juli cried, "the price you want for that little pinch of salt! What do you think I am?"

"What does he think you are, Miss Juli?" old Csipesz asked wonderingly and his voice was thicker than his waist. "Where do you have to go? I'll go instead, if you want me to!"

"Hush," someone whispered, "careful, or he'll hear you!"

István Kovács Jr. had placed himself outside the circle of guests, obviously to survey them all and dip them together

into the purifying bath of his happiness; he was standing some
twenty feet behind the fire leaning against the wall of the
office building and gripping two yards of railway sleeper that
had been in his hand ever since the fire was built. He was so
deeply engulfed by his contentment that even Juli's figure,
outlined by the fire, was constantly slipping from his attention. He bowed his head only, and a shallow furrow appeared
on his forehead when, now and again, the snub-nosed girl's
gaudy laughter rose shrill from the unicoloured conversation
of the company and hit him in the face.

"All right, all right, you don't have to be so riled, little
girl," the young man said in the sudden silence, "it's happened
to others before you. Here, take it, I'll let you have it for
nothing."

He pulled a small white package from his trouser pocket
and held it out to the girl. She tore it wordlessly from his
hand and immediately turned her back on him. Uncle
Csipesz bent over the package.

"What's that? . . . Salt?" he asked panting, pulling at his
beard with both hands. "And what does he want you to give
him for it? I'll go and give it to him, little Miss, you leave
it to me."

The little black cat on the red-headed woman's lap suddenly began to mew bitterly. "He's scared of the dogs,"
his mistress said, "and small wonder. All the mongrels of
Angyalföld must have assembled behind that fence . . . And
what do you think of this little slut? Swaggering like a
turkey-cock! Go on, neighbour, ask her at what convent she
was educated."

"Who is that young man?" asked the elderly, grey-
moustached carpenter sitting next to her who had lost all his

front teeth during the past year. "Has he worked here, at the lumber yard?"

"Not here," said Uncle Fecske pressing both hands on his stomach, or I'd know him."

"Well then, where does he work?"

"At a garage, I think."

"He's a chauffeur," the inn-keeper's wife confirmed. "He's called Feri Bellus. He isn't working there now. I know him from the shops, he lives next to us."

"Attractive kid," the red-headed woman said. "What am I to do with this cat? Where's he working now?"

"Nowhere, as far as I know," the inn-keeper's wife said. "He's bag-trading. Last time he brought some flour up from Pécs he offered it to me."

"For how much?"

The woman gave a resigned shrug.

"But what got into that little slut? What makes her act so proud?" the red-headed woman asked. "Nowadays there's nothing to get worked up about if a young man wants to go to bed with you. She can say no, and that's that."

"Perhaps she finds him too attractive," said the inn-keeper's wife, "and that is why she's so mad."

Apart from the old man racing about like a dog and István Kovács Jr. standing by the wall of the office building and watching his guests milling about from afar absorbedly as a shepherd watches his flock, the others pressed in an ever tightening, never loosening circle round the cooking meat, the increasingly enticing smell of onions and tasty steam of which made even the mouth of the most disciplined water. The grey-haired, clean-faced woman clasped her son's hand to calm him; the man's arm was shaking so much that she feared he would commit some unmannerly action in his wild voracity. Her own stomach tightened in a knot from the animal impulse of hunger and when, at times, the wind threw the onion-fragrant steam of the cauldron in her face, she almost collapsed; she felt an irresistible desire to snatch out the meat with her bare hands and tear it with her teeth, but we are human beings, she thought. The man sitting next but one to her on her left gnashed his teeth ceaselessly; she would have liked to stroke his hand, too, to calm him down. I hope there won't be any trouble, her heart contracted, the men will begin to drink and go berserk!

"Lucky he didn't hear it!" someone next to her said.

"What?"

"Well, the little bargain that Hitler-moustache offered the girl."

"What if he had heard?" the inn-keeper wanted to know.

"I wonder . . ." the woman shrugged her shoulder, "he looks like a mild man to me, but if he gets worked up . . . "

Bellus, who was sitting on a pile of boards close by, tossed his head and laughed at the woman with his perfect teeth.

"Then what?"

Nobody replied. The wind drove the smoke collecting under the cauldron into their faces and the inn-keeper coughed irritably.

"Stop that coughing, Uncle Csics," said Juli, who had her back to them but now suddenly turned to face them, "it would take just one word from me and he'd have settled his hash!"

"Whose hash?"

Bellus stroked his moustache.

"Do you mean mine?"

"Hush . . ." the grey-haired woman said, "hush! Don't bicker with your guests, Juli, my girl!"

"I wasn't coughing at you," the inn-keeper grumbled. "No use picking on me!"

The moon had risen, mixing its strident silver tones under the greying sky by the time the guests finished their dinner. The gentle evening wind that had at times flattened out the flames under the cauldron had dropped leaving in its train the cool vapours of the Danube; a stifling, acrid heat radiated from the stacks of wood that had condensed the full warmth of the day. An uninterrupted, confluent howl sounded from the street, from behind the wooden fence like the creaking of an overturned instrument; the dogs, maddened with hunger tore at the ground along the fence with foaming mouths, the dust rose high under their feet and floated over the fence in a thick cloud.

Dinner finished, the men stamped out the embers to ease the unbearable weight of the heat. Most of them were drunk already, the very first glass of wine had gone to their heads. The women drew aside into separate groups and railed against things as they were, throwing anxious glances at the men whose voices got more and more strident. In the centre of the moonlit yard the ten-year-old son of the inn-keeper and the snub-nosed, freckled girl were dancing holding each other by the waist. Juli ran over to István Kovács Jr. who had taken off his shirt immediately after dinner. He stood motionless in the same spot, in front of the office building, his trunk bare and glittering oily in the moonlight, clad in the animal cloth of his perspiration and with a gentle, satisfied smile on his lips. A thick lock of his flaxen hair tumbled over his forehead. He had eaten his dinner upright, thoroughly chewing every

mouthful of the tender, fraying meat that, with its wild and
tickly excitement reminded him of his childhood; then he
wiped his greasy mouth with the back of his hand, drank a
glass of wine, and went back to his shepherd's post near the
wall of the house from where he could watch over his guests'
well-being. His happiness was as steep and limpid as on the
night when he became Juli's lover.

"Why don't you join us, Cheshire Cat?" the girl asked,
flinging both arms round his neck.

"Yes, indeed," said the red-haired women who had gone
into the house to give her cat a drink, "why don't you join
us, Mr. Kovács? Aren't you afraid that someone might lure
this little girl away from you?"

"Me?" Juli laughed, "Me?" She raised herself on tip-toe
and pulling the giant's head down to her dropped a light kiss
on his mouth. "Me?"

"I prefer staying by myself," István Kovács Jr. said,
"because I look so frightening that everyone is scared of
me."

"Why should they be scared of you?"

"Ha-ha-ha,' Kovács Jr. laughed, "ha-ha-ha! What did you
say? Lure Juli away from me? What made you think such a
thing, lady?"

"There's no lack of candidates," the red-haired woman
informed him dropping her head gently.

By now the giant laughed so hard that all the women and
even some of the hotly arguing men turned their heads towards
them.

"Lure her away from me?" the giant thundered and tears
of laughter filled his eyes. "What makes you think that,
lady? . . . My Juli? We belong in one bed and one grave,

even our bones will rest together! What are you talking about, lady?"

"Shut up!" the girl whispered, blushing.

István Kovács Jr. slapped his thighs in his enormous good mood and tears flowed from his eyes.

"Don't slaver," Juli whispered in his ear furiously, "why must everybody see how happy you are?"

The giant put his arm round her waist.

"She wouldn't leave me if you put a rope round her neck, dear lady," he said lowering his voice because he noticed that some of the guests were coming towards them. "Not if you pulled! If anyone wants to, let them try, I won't hurt them!"

The red-headed woman turned pale. "You seem very sure of yourself, Mr. Kovács!"

The giant let go of Juli's waist, bent forward and gripped the woman's shoulders with both hands.

"No living being has ever betrayed me yet," he said slowly sinking his humid, blue gaze into the woman's eyes, "neither carnivorous not herbivorous, do you get me, dear lady?"

By now five or six men were standing around them and some of the women were approaching.

"Try what?" a voiced asked.

Juli turned round suddenly as if a snake had bitten her in the ankle.

"What is it we're to try, Mr. Kovács?"

"Whether or not Juli could be enticed away from him," the red-headed woman explained to Bellus who had come to her side. "Because I told him that . . ."

"Every woman can be seduced," the inn-keeper's wife declared in a decisive voice. Already the first glass of wine excited her to such a degree that she had let down her hair and kicked off her shoes.

"That's not quite true . . ."

"It is true," the inn-keeper's wife cried. "Every one of them; one has only got to know how! I've seen many a thing with these two eyes of mine, Mr. Hanak. Today, for instance, there is no woman one couldn't buy for a kilo of white flour!"

"One kilo?"

The grey-haired, toothless cabinet-maker shook his head. "She's pretty high, this one," he said disgruntled, "someone should take her home!"

"I'd be glad to pay a kilo of flour for Juli," the bare-footed lad in the military trousers whispered next to him, "could you lend a little money, Mr. Hanak?"

The cabinet-maker made no reply.

"I'd wash my feet into the bargain, Uncle!"

For a second there was silence; István Kovács Jr. raised his white-fluffed hand.

"I don't know what you think of the world," he said in a unexpectedly low voice turning to the inn-keeper's wife, "because I don't understand this kind of talk. All I know is that no one has ever betrayed me yet. Why should you think that someone might lure Juli away from me?"

The woman blushed red.

"What did you say, Mr. Kovács?"

"Quiet!" the giant commanded, "I have something more to say. Take a look at this girl, lady! Is she the sort of girl who can be taken away from me?"

A low, quickly suppressed giggle sounded from the edge of the little group and the giant tilted his head in amazement.

"Who was that?" he asked.

"Shut up!" Juli shouted blood-red in the face, "shut up right now or I am going!"

"Never mind him, girl," the inn-keeper's wife said to her mockingly, "he's a good man even if he is a bit cracked in the head."

István Kovács Jr. turned to her.

"What did you whisper, Aunty Csics? Who is not supposed to hear you?"

"I said ..." the woman who felt her blood go to her head in her confusion, "I said, Mr. Kovács, that every woman can be seduced!"

"What?" a voice next to her exclaimed, "Even in our democracy?"

"Even Juli, Aunty?" the lad in the military trousers asked slyly, "Mr. Kovács' Juli?"

"You've got to pay her price, that's all, Mr. Kovács," the inn-keeper's wife continued more and more savagely, "because every one of them has her price however much she may deny it!"

"Can the price be paid in pengoes?"

"In dollars, love!" a voice screamed in the back, "that's the new Hungarian currency!"

"What do you want with that silly giant!" someone said aloud.

In the meantime most of the small groups talking further away had come to join the crowd arguing outside the office building, shuffling in the freshly strewn, moonlit sawdust with the intoxication of meat and wine in their nerves, their faces livid, their foreheads covered in perspiration. Only the revellers remained in the open stretch near the gate: Uncle

Fecske, who, dinner over, had immediately brought out his
fiddle, a baker's assistant with his fiancée, a lame soldier, a
widow with a big bone, gnawed clean, in her hand, and the
inn-keeper's ten-year-old son who, with his arms around the
freckled girl's waist was revolving around his own axis his
eyes closed, panting, half-faint, butting his head from time
to time with the wild movement of a young goat into the tall
girl's belly. Behind the dancers, leaning against a pile of
boards, a fat, legless beggar sat on the ground in a German
army blouse, clapping the rhythm wildly under the feet of
the dancers.

"Unbutton your blouse," the baker's assistant whispered
pressing his lips to his fiancée's ear, "unbutton your blouse!"
The girl giggled drunkenly and shook her head.

"You don't believe me, Mr. Kovács," the inn-keeper's
wife screeched, "and you'll pay for it one day! Where
were you during the war that you remained so innocent?"

"I was at home, at Barcs," the giant replied quietly. "I
worked at the lumber yard. I'll be only eighteen this
autumn."

"You don't say!"

"Are you that old?" the lad in the military trousers asked
and spat on the ground. "I thought you weren't a day over
fourteen!"

The red-headed woman broke into loud laughter. "Then
it isn't surprising that you aren't more experienced as far as
women are concerned," she said. "Don't worry, you'll
learn in Budapest. But take good care of your Juli if you
want to keep her for a while."

"For how long?" someone asked.

"Let's say a month or two."

"That long?" a voice wondered. "Hell, we're not in the provinces!"

The violin fell suddenly silent among the group of dancers, there was a druken female scream followed by a hoarse oath.

"What's going on there?" the toothless, grey-haired cabinet-maker asked turning back started. The inn-keeper's wife laughed.

"They want someone to unbutton something. They are having quite a time with that button... Apparently it's done..." he added lewdly when, a second later, the violin struck up again and the swearing man fell silent. "Let's go see what they are doing, coming, Mr. Kovács?"

But apparently the giant had heard nothing of the passionate, brief intermezzo; he stared ahead deep in thought, his chin resting on his chest, only at his name did he raise his head.

"*Shto se ljutis na mene?*" he said quietly.

"What did you say?" the inn-keeper's wife asked.

"When I was a child that's how I asked my mother why she was angry with me," István Kovács Jr. said musingly. "It's Serbian. Why are you all angry with me?"

In the sudden silence people looked at each other and a woman broke into a forced laugh. Juli, who had drawn to the edge of the group where she stood burning with shame and silent, now stepped up to István Kovács Jr. and put her hand on his arm.

"Be quite, Cheshire Cat, don't talk to them," she said aloud for everyone to hear, "they don't deserve it."

"Why shouldn't they deserve it?" the giant asked. "I know they are angry with me because I am stronger than they are, but that's not my fault, is it?"

The heat was almost unbearable, the toothless cabinet-

maker took off his shirt. "Now what does that Hitler
moustache want again?" he asked anxiously when his head
reappeared from under the shirt. They all looked at Bellus
who had stepped suddenly from the semi-circle flashing his
white teeth. He sunk both hands into his trouser pockets
and the light of the full moon combed his oily black hair
into tiny, saucy waves. But the giant threw him no more
than a glance, then he yawned deeply and contentedly, spread
wide his arms and stretched luxuriously.

"I'll tell you something, Mr. Kovács!" Bellus cried casting
a challenging glance at the girl who stared with rounded eyes,
aghast, back to him. People fidgeted nervously and the grey-
haird, clean-faced woman grasped her son's arm that had
again begun to shake. "I'll tell you something!"

The giant nodded.

"You are very sure of yourself, aren't you, Mr. Kovács?"

The giant nodded again.

'Well, if you are so sure," Bellus continued smiling and his
voice turned only a shade sharper, "if you are so sure that
Miss Juli cannot be swept off her feet, then let her come
home with me tonight."

Behind them the violin left off again, there was no other
sound but the growling of the dogs scratching the ground
outside the fence. The silent yard was full of the smell of
meat and wine. A shot was heard from afar, which seemed
to propogate a second and then, a third.

"Well, Mr. Kovács?" Bellus asked smiling.

The inn-keeper's wife was the first to regain her breath;
she broke into loud laughter in her deep, hoarse voice.

"He is right," she cried, "If you are so sure of yourself,
Mr. Kovács, let her go with him!"

The red-haired woman pressed both hands on her abdomen in her nervousness. "That's it!" she screamed her voice cracking, "Why shouldn't he let her go? He has nothing to worry about!"

"Yes, do let her go," screeched the bare-footed lad in the army trousers, "I'll go along and make sure that nothing happens to them!"

"The question is: where does he live?"

"I'll go along no matter how far!"

"He lives quite near here," sounded a faltering male voice.

"Well, then there's no reason why he shouldn't let her go."

"Sure," the lad yelled, "that'll save her getting tired and she can defend herself better when they get there!"

The drunken laughter of the inn-keeper's wife flashed to and fro like a conductor's baton above the medley of loud voices. "He lives with his mother, Mr. Kovács!" she screamed at the top of her voice, "You can let her go safely!"

"No doubt about it!" the lad shouted, "If he lives with his mother I don't even have to accompany them!"

"Mr. Kovács," the red-headed woman yelled sinking her fingers into her neighbour's shoulders, "now we shall see if you trust her or not!"

"That's it!" cried several voices, "Now we'll see!"

"Will you let her go?"

The silence that followed the question cast out within a second every neutral noise: the sound of the violin and the growling of the dogs outside seemed to have been swallowed up by the water. The giant raised his head and looked at his tormentors.

But before he could open his mouth the young locksmith with the stoop whom nobody knew and who now spoke for the first time in the course of the evening, stepped out of the semi-circle and planted himself in front of Bellus.

"Scoundrel!" he said in a loud voice tilting his head a little to one side.

The chauffeur measured him with his eyes. "What's your gripe?" he said curtly.

"All I say is that you are a scoundrel!" the young man repeated. "And you are a a lot of stinkers, damn you to hell!" he shouted towards the others shaking his fists at them, then he turned on his heel and set out towards the gate.

Bellus caught up with him in two leaps, grasped his shoulders and turned him round.

"What did you say, comrade?" he asked smiling. "Would you repeat it?"

"Scoundrel!" yelled the locksmith beside himself with rage, "scoundrel!"

Bellus hit him in the face with his fist, then picked him up by the waist and, with terrific force, threw the collapsing body yards away, where, with a dull thud, it landed on the ground. By the time the red-headed woman began to scream, he was back in his place, carefully smoothing down with his palm first his shiny hair, then his tiny black moustache. "Quiet!" he told the woman in a low voice. She obeyed. "Well, Mr. Kovács, what do you think of the test I suggested?"

The grey-haired woman took her son's hand. "Let's get out of this," she whispered, "it isn't decent that we should eat his food and then make fun of him!"

"Then why is he such an idiot?" murmured the lad in the army trousers and belched loudly. The old cabinet-maker standing next to them turned turkey-red, slapped the lad,

then walked away quickly towards the lifeless body lying by
the fence.

"Well, Mr. Kovács," Bellus's voice rose again, "Will you
allow Miss Juli to come with me?"

The giant stood motionless by the house wall and turned
his head right and left in amazement. His lips were half open
and almost imperceptibly trembling; there was no other
sign to show that he understood what was going on around
him. The large, smooth planes of his face remained just as
untouched as the yards long log clasped in his two palms;
only his flaxen hair sparkled passionately as if, with every
angry cell, it wanted to quarrel with the wild, mineral glitter
of the moon.

"István!" Juli screamed frightened, pressing her palm on
her mouth.

At the girl's voice the giant's face came to life. It drew
into a slight grimace as if he were about to laugh, the nail-
sized brown wart at the tip of his left brow began to tremble,
he meditated for a moment, then his neck turned suddenly
dark, his tiny snub-nose flickered, his eyes narrowed.

"What did you say?" he asked barely audibly.

The first row began to back away, the red-headed woman's
high heel dug into the inn-keeper's wife's bare foot. Not a
breath disturbed the silence. The lad tightened his fists so
hard in his excitement that his nails drew blood. Bellus too
retreated a little but immediately afterwards he stepped
forward again.

István Kovács Jr. glanced up at the sky, then he grasped the
two ends of the sleeper and pressed it down on his thigh. His
face turned slowly black. When the wood began to crack
the red-headed woman turned and set out running towards

the gate. The grey-haired woman dragged her son by his
arm after her, the inn-keeper swore in a low voice and took
hold of his wife whose cheeks had gone livid with terror,
pushing her by the shoulder towards the gate. The lad in
the army trousers retched while running. Uncle Fecske's
fiddle had also fallen silent and the fat, legless beggar fled in
huge leaps, like a giant frog, towards the exit, supporting
himself on the wooden soles fitted to his hands.

By the time the sleeper broke in two with a sharp crack
and the giant straightened up reeling, only Bellus faced him
alone in the moonlit square. The chauffeur looked into his
eyes, then he bent his head, thrust both hands into his trouser
pockets and, whistling, set out towards the gate. Kovács Jr.
dropped the two pieces of wood and ran towards the centre
of the yard. Their tails between their legs, their ears flattened,
the dogs stole in by the open gate and threw themselves
yelping on the scattered pieces of bone. A huge, bushy-
tailed sheep-dog that raced to and fro across the moonlit
square like a ghost, bit through the throats of two smaller
dogs. The area in front of the office building resounded all
night with the barking of the crazed animals.

As soon as she recovered from her faint, Juli began to look
for the hiding giant. The big lumber-yard stretched all the
way down to the Danube, she had to search the innumerable
tiny streets between the tall stacks of lumber, the store where
the tiles of wood were kept, the log-sawing shop, the kilo-
metre long fence. When she had shouted herself hoarse, she
would crouch down on a plank and cry softly until the tall,
white-bearded figure of Uncle Csipesz, ambling after her,
appeared between two shadows and chased her on with his
raised forefinger. At times she would stop and sing the song

of their love that the giant had taught her in the first days of their happinness. "Cheshire Cat!" she cried, "Listen!"

"Eheu fugaces, Postume Postume. . . ."

She fell silent and strained her ears.

"Answer me!" she shouted into the humming, silver-spotted night, "Sing with me!"

"Labuntur anni nec pietas moram
Rugis et instanti senecta
Adferet indomitaeque morti."

She found him towards dawn behind a big pile of boards. He was crying, his face pressed into the ground. Juli sat down next to him and put both arms around his huge shoulders his tears ran down her neck.

"Sweet Cheshire Cat, my love," she sobbed, "I don't want to betray you."

István Kovács Jr. and his Juli were starving. The foodstuffs coming to the capital from the countryside were not being sold for money; they changed owners for gold or cloth. Juli possessed nothing but a single blouse apart from her thin dress and Kovács Jr. owned one pair of trousers and two ragged shirts; they had nothing but their youth to exchange for a side of bacon. The weekly wages provided the maize-bread and, at times, a dish of cabbage. They had to look around for some earnings.

Few factories were in operation in Angyalföld yet and there were scarcely any street-cars. At times an odd lorry would sweep along the deserted Vác Avenue into which the side streets on both sides pumped nothing but their sunlit silence. When the tired shadow of a lone pedestrian crept up the walls of the houses it lingered there like a meditating spider only to creep on after a while in alarm and drop to the ground on the corner. Weeds grew between the flagstones and last year's posters yawned on the fences. In the evening the streets cooled and by the time it grew dark only the rats devoured their sole food: silence, amidst the mildewed walls of the deserted factory buildings.

Uncle Fecske's weak old age yielded to the hunger: one morning, when his only shirt disintegrated in his hands, he lay back on his straw mattress and died. Kovács Jr. found him the same day. As the old man hadn't grumbled around the house for a few days, he went to fetch him himself at the guard's house standing at the other end of the lumber yard. There was a small sun-drenched lawn in front of the little red-brick building overshadowed on right and left by tall wood piles; its single, blistered window stared unblinking into the afternoon sun. A solitary rat scrambled from the threshold as the giant's boots stepped into the silence.

Kovács Jr. stopped before the closed door and listened with his head bent. The buzzing of wild bees wove a net above the sunlit area, the smell of dry lumber blended with the spicy perfume of mint. The giant listened with baited breath; a second stillness lay behind the silence. He pushed in the door with his index finger and, glancing slowly around the little room, took stock of death.

The two worn, torn shoes stood under the bed with their toes towards darkness. The setting sun sent an oblique ray into the one closer to the window, lighting up the absence of the old, bunioned foot. Next to the bed, on the woven straw seat of a chair, a little soapy water glittered in a chipped

enamelled bowl, its grey bubbles glancing now and again at
their master lying in the bed. On a small table next to the
wall stood the picture of a woman, in front of it bread-crumbs
and a half-closed knife. Both doors of the wardrobe stood
open, it was completely empty. When, at times, the wind
blew in by the open door it received no answer from the
inside; there was no tablecloth on the table, no sheet on the
straw mattress that could have waved back. In the bed
there was no breathing.

Kovács Jr. flung out the dirty water in the basin, poured
clean water into it, then he undressed and washed the body.
As he possessed no comb and found none in the old man's
pocket, he smoothed down the grey hair and moustache with
his palm. He worked with very tender, gentle fingers as if
he was afraid of causing the old man pain. He put the pipe
he found on the floor near the bed into the dead man's hand
so that he could take the only possession he had acquired in a
lifetime with him into the earth.

"Well, Uncle, and what am I to do with you now?" he
asked sadly, sitting down on the edge of the bed. "There's
no one to keep vigil, so the rats will eat you."

He shook his head.

"He's as helpless as the day his mother dropped him into
the world. What's the use of living if you can't even produce
a child to close your eyes on your death bed. I'll have so
many, Uncle, that there won't be enough room on my lap."

He burst out laughing and placed his huge palm on the
dead man's bare breast.

"You mind, don't you, that it's over?" he asked pausing
curiously as if expecting the dead man to answer. "The
Danube doesn't care what he flows into in the end, only what

countries he flows through. And it doesn't hurt him to get some slops in the neck now and again, it doesn't make him lose courage."

He rose from the bed and stood at the door. The sun had dropped down between the Buda mountains, painting the stationary fleecy clouds that embraced the western horizon like a huge, quiet wreath, a fiery red. The chimneys of the Obuda factories loomed black and smokeless above the purple background, like senseless exclamation marks on the course of an unwritten sentence, and below them the Danube rolled along, with fertile, russet brilliance, its summer-night waves mixed with filth, anger, blood and joy. The giant raised his head and, his chest expanding, gazed open-eyed at the landscape. His confidence in life was so strong that suffering left no deeper mark on him than the shadow of a cloud on the water, and happiness had penetrated every particle of his being to such an extent that he forgot the dead man as soon as he turned his back on him and only his nerves retained in their vibration Uncle Fecske's memory slowly dissolving in the dusk. It was already dark when Juli's light steps brought him back to reality.

"Where have you been, Cheshire Cat?" the girl asked anxiously. "It's night! Whom are you guarding here?"

Kovács Jr. wiped his eyes with his fist.

"I didn't even know I was crying," he said amazed.

The girl bent close to his face.

"Are you crying?"

"The old man died," the giant said. "But I don't think that's what is making me cry... We must take him home with us or the rats will eat him."

He carried the light, old body home in his arms but as

Juli refused to sleep in the same room with it he laid it out on a wide, thick pine-board in the area in front of the office building and lay down next to it on the ground. He was tired and hungry.

"Juli!" he shouted into the house, "give me something to eat!"

"What do you want?" he heard her after a while.

"Give me something to eat!" the giant repeated.

The girl stood naked in the doorway. "At this hour?" she said uncertainly. "You want me to make up the fire in the middle of the night? And you want to eat there, beside the body?"

"Why not?" the giant asked uncomprehending. "Why shouldn't I eat next to him? I live, so I have to eat!"

The girl raised herself on tip-toe and threw an alarmed glance at the body.

"Well, I couldn't eat now!" she cried impatiently. The giant wagged his head.

"A pity," he said. "Still, you can give me something."

Juli threw herself aginst the door-frame, her white lucent body shaking with angry weeping. "How could I," she sobbed panting, "when there isn't a slice of bread in the house. Where do you want me to get it if you don't bring any! We'll starve to death like this old man! Look!"

She ran on tip-toe to the body and squatted down by it.

"Look at his ribs," she whispered, "you can tell he died of starvation!"

Kovács Jr. bent over the corpse. The ribs protuded from the body in sharp lines and below them the sunken belly descended towards the loins like a deep, black ditch. The pointed nose, grown to twice its size, rose steep from the waxy yellow face; in the light of the rising moon it threw an oblique shadow on the sunken cheek and the flat-edged yoke-bone towering above it. The upper lip had slid up a little baring the yellow gleam of the upper denture; it seemed as if he were snarling at the sky. The giant threw Juli an anxious look. But the motionless girl squatting naked with her long waist rising from her hips, and her breasts gleaming stiff in the moonlight, calmed his heart like the evening flute coming up from the banks of the Drava in his childhood; she was indescribably sweet, flexible and exciting and cradled the melody of a whole life in the light and shade of her white body.

"Come here to me!" the giant said.

The day, after the funeral, Kovács Jr. went to work at the cable-factory of P. where the workers had already begun rebuilding the plant. He was taken on as a navvy to clear away the rubble. At home, Uncle Fecske's place was taken by the long-bearded Uncle Csipesz who watched the lumber-yard with Juli by day and with whom they had always shared their food—when they had any. The weekly wages didn't go far, for money had no teeth in those days, all it brought to the house was some carrots, cabbages, maize flour and apricots—but at times the factory committee would distribute a litre of oil, a kilogram of beans, Hungarian rice; they brought potatoes up from the countryside and on one occasion they sweetened a descending Saturday night with half a kilo of sugar.

Kovács Jr. rose at dawn and got home late at night. He stood with a heavy heart in the darkness before the locked and barricaded gate listening, his head bent, to the double silence before and behind it. Juli sang more rarely now.

When he asked her what had made her lark's mood go dry she shook her head, laughed at him and the flash of her white teeth wiped the wrinkles off the giant's heart in a moment, but still, the next evening it was again with a contracting heart that he stopped before the gate and thought long, frowning, before hammering on the silence of the yard.

One evening he was again greeted by singing. It was an absentminded, low humming: as if the girl were sitting behind the fence, waiting. At his gentle knock the iron bolt creaked.

"Shall I let you in?" he heard the girl's voice.

"Please!" the giant replied happily.

"What have you brought me?"

"Nothing."

"Nothing?" the girl cried, "Then I won't let you in."

"Do let me in," Kovács Jr. said entreatingly.

"Kneel down on the ground and beg me to!" the girl demanded.

Kovács Jr. grinned broadly at the locked gate.

"I won't beg you," he said, "because I did bring you something."

There was silence and the giant watched the motionless gate tensely.

"Show me what you brought," he suddenly heard Juli's voice above his head, "show me, or I won't let you in."

The giant looked up startled. "How did you get up there?"

The girl's head peeped out into the street above the tall wooden fence and somewhat lower down her toes wriggled in one of the mouldy holes in the board. "By lift," Juli said. "Show me what you've brought!"

It was a dark, starless night; soon it began to rain. After dinner Juli climbed onto István Kovács Jr.'s lap.

"Will you marry me?" she asked. "This morning, when I went to the office of the lumber company to collect your wages they asked me whether I was your wife. What could I say?"

"What did you say?" the giant asked, his voice squeaky with excitement. "The director told me that if I made good now . . ."

He fell silent and looked alarmed into the girl's face. "I can't recall what he promised if I made good," he said surprised. "It was the day I got meat from the Russians and in the evening . . ."

He dropped his head into his hands. "What's happened to me?" he sighed. "What has happened? Lately . . . I forget everything . . ." He pressed the girl's burning body to his chest. "I remember only you . . . nothing else in the world! I'll write to Barcs tomorrow, shall I?"

"What for?" the girl asked.

"For my papers" the giant said in a low voice. "So I can marry you and have as many children from you as the evening wind will sigh tonight. Count those sighs, Juli."

The trains came and went rarely; irregularly, mail arrived at snail's pace. After the first week Juli would stand at the gate to watch for the postman turning the corner from the direction of Vác Avenue but after another week she grew tired of the hopeless game and in the evening Kovács Jr. was again met by the old, songless silence. The girl lost not only her high spirits but also the roundness of her cheeks, her brown eyes flashed and, as if she were exhausted, her voice lost its timbre, her walk its springiness: and she became less talkative. One evening she opened the gate to Kovács Jr. with a cigarette between her lips. He stopped in his tracks and stared, agape at the glowing butt.

"Is that you, Juli," he asked breathlessly, "I didn't know you smoked!"

"Won't you marry me if I do?" the girl murmured her voice vibrating with nervousness. "There is a lot you don't know!"

"What don't I know?" the giant asked quietly.

"Nothing."

The giant bent closer.

"What's the matter, Juli?" he asked with infinite tenderness.

"Nothing," the girl shook her head. "At least nothing more than that there isn't any supper. I got three cigarettes for my money. Because this government of yours can only talk big, it's too dumb to give the people bread."

A few days later she was again smoking a cigarette; she got it from the Russians who, she told him, had knocked at the gate for a glass of water but then stayed on half the afternoon. She hadn't been afraid of them, she flashed Kovács Jr. a wicked glance, nor did they harm her. On the contrary, they left her a box of cigarettes for her hospitality. They even invited her to the Urania to see a Russian film.

"Why didn't you go?" the giant asked. "If you could have got home in time . . ."

One morning an unexpected guest showed up at the lumber yard, Aunty Csics, the inn-keeper's wife. Uncle Csipez, who was raking through his beard near the gate, let her in.

"Send the old man away, girl," the woman winked at Juli, "I want to talk to you alone," She bent to the girl's ear. "I've brought you a message from Feri Bellus!"

The girl turned almost imperceptibly paler, the rings around her eyes became a shade darker and softer.

"I'm not interested!" she said.

Aunty Csics smiled. "Bellus asked me to tell you that he is sorry."

Juli shook her head. "I'm not interested," she informed the woman. "I'm not playing ... What do you want Uncle Csipesz?"

The lanky old man was standing behind them, digging his bearded goat-head between the shoulders of the two women.

"What does she want here?" he asked threateningly pointing his bony fore-finger at the inn-keeper's wife. "What is she doing here, Miss Juli? Did you ask her to come?"

Aunty Csics burst into annoyed laughter. "Go to hell, you old billy-goat!"

"Where do you want me to go?" the old man asked. "What did you say, where am I to go?"

His long white beard fluttered with surprise. "Why are you sending me away?" he asked plaintively. "I've never stolen in my life, not even a piece of bread, though I've lived to a very old age, Miss Juli. And now you are sending me to hell!"

"All right," Juli said, "we are not going to hurt you, Uncle Csipesz! But now put your beard back in its place and clear out!"

But suddenly the old man straightened up and pointed his forefinger again at Aunty Csics.

"Don't allow her into the house," he shouted in his thunderous bass, "because this woman comes straight from Satan's throne and she infects the ground she treads on. If

you let her cross your threshold, Miss Juli, the days of anguish
have begun, for this woman carries war and abomination in
her clothes!"

"Bless my soul, you really got him going!" Juli said
amazed when the old man's bent back disappeared behind
the nearest stack of boards. "I've never seen him so worked
up!"

The inn-keeper's wife placed her shopping bag on the
floor and lifted a huge, golden-red loaf of bread from it.

"Feri sent this," she said laying the loaf into Juli's arms
like a smiling baby, "It is pure wheat, my child. And he
apologizes to you and your husband."

"My husband?" Juli asked.

"What, you aren't married yet?" the woman throwing
up her hands in astonishment. "We thought that as you
were so happy together . . ."

The girl was looking down rigid and motionless at the
bread in her arms. "How much does it weigh?" she asked
with an unconscious smile. But suddenly she turned pale and
her forehead sprang into wrinkles.

"Take it away!" she said. "Take it back to him!"

"He doesn't want anything from you," the woman
explained, "he doesn't care if he never sees you again in this
life. He is ashamed of having annoyed you so much and he
wants to be forgiven, that's all."

Juli shook her head. "No, go! Take it from me."

But Aunty Csics had already turned away. "You can't
refuse it," she called back over her shoulders, "except in your
own name, my heart! But as he sent it to both of you, I
certainly won't take it back!"

The girl's arm twitched as if to fling the bread after her

but her mother-instinct held back the movement—one doesn't throw away living life! When Kovács Jr. returned in the evening the loaf of bread was still lying on the table, uncut.

The giant stopped in the door and, stretching his neck forward, stared at the bread motionless for a few seconds. Then suddenly he emitted a loud yell and reached the table in one leap. The shipdeck boards creaked under his down-coming soles as if the earth were trembling below them. He gathered up the bread from the table and giving another, even louder yell, pressed it to his bosom. He crushed it wildly as if he wanted to wrestle with it and with one single, huge embrace, assimilate it into his own body. The muscles rippled thick on his two arms that completely concealed the bread, the veins of his neck stood out, his long, flaxen hair tumbled over his forehead. But only for a second did the cruel impulse obscure his face; after the second yell, when his chest had again sunk back between his ribs and the hissing breath abated in his mouth, he broke, unexpectedly, into a smile and, cradling the loaf in his arm, he began slowly to dance.

"La-la-la-la" he hummed circling around the table and his eyes rested as ecstatically on the bread as if a whole summery wheat-field were whispering in it. Once he stopped in his gyrations, threw the loaf high into the air so that it almost brushed the ceiling, then he caught it in his two upheld arms and pressed it, with a low murmur, to his face.

When he had overturned the second chair with his intoxicated feet, Juli, who had retreated, frightened, into a corner, whence, covered in goose-pimples, she watched the dancing giant, suddenly lost her temper, jumped in front of him and sank both her hands in his hair.

"Stop!" she cried furiously, "or I'll run away so far that you'll never find me again as long as you live!"

István Kovács Jr. bent over the girl's face.

"You are right," he said panting, 'I'll stop in a minute, I'll make only one more round . . .'"

Juli stamped her feet angrily. "Not even once!"

"All right," Kovács Jr. said. "You know, Juli, I thought I was back home. Let me have the knife."

He sat down on the threshold, his legs wide apart, drew the knife four times over the edge of the stone-step, wiped it in his palm, then he made the sign of the cross on the loaf and cut it. He chewed slowly, rhythmically, brushing away with the back of his hand the crumbs that stuck to his chin. Juli sat opposite him on a bench and watched him silently, her eyes flashing.

"Who did you get it from?" Kovács Jr. asked, his mouth full.

The girl turned away her head.

"When you have eaten your fill I'll tell you."

The giant forgot to swallow.

"What did you say?" he asked munching, "Why don't you tell me who gave it to you?"

"The Russians . . ." Juli said.

Kovács Jr. continued to eat.

"God bless them," he grumbled. "How much does it weigh?"

"It must have weighed about three kilos," Juli said. "My guess would be it can't weigh more than a pound now."

"Have I eaten so much of it?" Kovác Jr. said amazed, "Yet I only started a quarter of an hour ago . . . But then there's hardly any left for you!"

"Hardly," muttered Juli.

Kovács Jr. cut the remainder in half and put one half into Juli's lap.

"Let's finish it," he suggested and already the next slice crunched under his teeth. "There's no point in saving it for tomorrow, is there?"

A week later Aunty Csics showed up again; this time she brought a little flour and a jar of lard—but Bellus' name wasn't even mentioned. If Juli was resolved not to accept it free of charge, she could let her have a little fire-wood for the winter, it wouldn't diminish the vast sea of wood, she said looking around, if they scooped up a couple of jugfuls of its water. On the other hand it would do them both good to put a little flesh on their rattling frames. She patted Juli's cheek.

"You've grown so thin, child," she said, "that it hurts to look at you. Have you got married yet?"

The girl turned her head away.

"The papers haven't arrived yet."

"They will arrive sooner or later, isn't it true?" the inn-keeper's wife nodded. "It isn't necessary for him to know that you are doing a little bartering behind his back. If a man cannot look after himself, then his woman must, at least with her left hand."

The evenings were growing cooler, darkness fell early. After letting out the inn-keeper's wife, Juli went back into the room and, crouching on the straw mattress in the descending night, examined her big toe until it disappeared completely in the dark. Uncle Csipesz was snoozing on a chair in the corner, wheezing raggedly at Death circling above his head on slow pinions.

That day Kovács Jr. returned home earlier than usual. "Why don't you light the lamp?" he asked stepping into the dark room.

Juli climbed back on to the straw mattress.

"Have you brought some kerosene?"

"Where could I have brought kerosene from?" the giant asked, shamefaced.

"From the kerosene sea ... a hatful?' Juli grumbled. "Where from? How do I know where from! From the factory where you work!"

"There's no kerosene there," Kovács Jr. shook his head. "Give me some food."

Juli's greenish cat's eyes became almost luminous in her sudden fury.

"God damn this miserable democracy!" she shouted hitting the straw mattress with both fists, God damn it, to hell with all its thieving ministers! Let the workers swallow his spittle ... but they, they can sell the country and grow fat on the yield! Where do they take all the kerosene and the pigs and the wheat there was in this country ... tell me that!"

Kovács Jr. held out both arms towards the girl.

"What is it, Juli?" he asked mildly, "what has happened to you?"

"Answer me," the girl cried, hitting the straw mattress again with all her force, "tell me why you are working for nothing with that huge body of yours? For whom are you working without pay? Who gobbles up everything you earn with your work?"

"Juli, sweet," the giant begged with joined hands, "calm down! How should I know who ..."

But before he could have finished the sentence Juli jumped in front of him in a long leap, placed her bare feet on his boots and, sinking her ten fingers into his shoulder, began to shake Kovács Jr.

"Do you want to eat?" she screamed beside herself with rage, "What shall I give you? Did you bring something? And if you did, am I to cook it in the dark? Or did you bring kerosene and matches to make up the fire? And did you bring salt for me to season the nothing that you brought? What can I give you to eat?"

Uncle Csipesz who had been sitting silent and motionless in the corner suddenly rose, yawned deeply and left the room. Juli turned her head and looked after him.

"This one too will perish in my hands," she said turning pale, "but what do you care?" "If I wanted to trade a couple of cartfuls of lumber from the yard for some food, I bet you wouldn't let me!"

"Juli," the giant said, "that wood doesn't belong to us! How you talk! Tell me, who've you been seeing lately? There's a different smell to your talk!"

At this minute, breaking into the silence of the night, a loud hammering was heard from the direction of the gate. Juli let go of the giant's shoulder and jumped back.

"Jesus," she whispered and the alarm in her voice showed up her face in so strong a light that through the darkness Kovács Jr. could make out even the gleam of her wide eyes and the wild flash of her teeth. "Cheshire Cat, don't let anyone in!"

But the bolt was alreading creaking and the rusty sound of the hinges made a deep scratch on the nocturnal calm of the lumber yard.

The rain-drenched sawdust swallowed the noise of steps, only Uncle Csipesz's excited panting approached in the darkness.

"I wonder who he's let in?" said the giant.

"Jesus," the girl whispered, "I forgot to bolt it properly and Uncle Csipesz lets anyone in!"

"Who is that?" Juli cried. "Who is that with you, Uncle Csipesz?"

"I wish you a good evening," it came from the threshold, "It's me, Feri Bellus. Have you gone to bed already?"

The room made no reply. The next second the yellow cone of light from a pocket torch penetrated the room and extricated Juli's and Kovács Jr.'s faces from the darkness.

"Forgive me for intruding on you at this hour," Bellus said, "but as I know that Mr. Kovács goes to work during the day I didn't want to come earlier. Miss Juli, wouldn't you light the lamp?"

"I have no kerosene," Juli said. "What do you want?"

"Give me the lamp," Bellus's voice sounded now from near the table.

Juli stepped back. "I don't want it!" she said almost inaudibly. But the screw of the lamp was already creaking and kerosene counted the seconds with a greasy clucking. The flame of the match jumped on to the wick, flared up, then subsided and radiated a yellow light under the clinking cylinder. Bellus stroked down his moustache with two illuminated fingers.

"How did you know?" Juli stammered.

"I didn't. I just had some with me."

"Go away!" the girl screamed, "go away!"

"Pardon me," Bellus said clamly, "I would have come

earlier to apologize to you, but I had to go on a trip. I am sorry, Mr. Kovács, that I spoiled your party last time."

The giant stood motionless near the table, his arms hanging, with his less compact shadow running up to the ceiling behind his back. His face shone waxy in the light illuminating it from below, his small eyes were dead, like holes punched in the dark. Juli threw him a quick, inquisitive glance then, almost imperceptibly, drew away from him.

"I didn't want to offend you," Bellus said in his deep, dark voice, "let's forget it, Mr. Kovács."

The giant put both hands behind his back.

"Must you be so implacable?"

Juli drew even further back. The giant brought his arms forward and laid both open palms on his chest.

"I don't know how to forget," he said bowing his head.

Bellus broke into a smile. "Do try! Miss Juli, won't you come to my aid?"

"I don't know how to forget," the giant repeated. "In here everything keeps alive as if it were imprinted on my heart. Can I help that, Mr. Bellus?"

"Well," Bellus smiled and his teeth flashed, "If you can't, you can't, that shouldn't prevent us from being friends, am I right, Miss Juli?" He held out his open palm towards the giant. "Put it there!"

"No," the giant said.

Bellus blushed a deep red but his teeth continued to flash.

"Right, Mr. Cheshire Cat," he said mockingly, "I wanted to team up with you so we can travel together to the country, but if this is how it is . . . Miss Juli, do you bear a grudge too?"

"What do you want, Uncle Csipesz?" the girl cried at that minute. The old man had jumped from his chair and was advancing, stumbling, towards them, his arm extended, his index finger pointing at Bellus.

"I forbid it!" Juli shouted, "Do you hear me, I forbid it!"

The old man stopped in his tracks.

"Are you a married man?" he boomed at Bellus in his thunderous bass.

The young man laughed at him and shook his head. "I'm a bachelor like yourself, Uncle Csipesz!"

"Right!" the old man boomed, "but are you fornicating, the Lord asks? Do you drink? Do you smoke? ... Can you hear heaven throbbing overhead? Answer and remember that it will come down on your sinful head and kill you if you don't reply truthfully to the Lord's question!"

Outside a splashing rain came down on the ground and a flash of lightning threw a yellow light on the yard beyond the window.

"I must admit that I smoke, Uncle Csipesz," Bellus said. "I know it is a sin, but to hell with it! What else do you want to know, dad?"

The old man directed his bony, yellow index finger towards Juli.

"Do you love this maiden?" he shouted at the top of his voice to outdo the crack of the thunderbolt. "For if you love her, let me prophesy that the day of Armageddon has come on which good and evil go into battle for the possession of the lamb; they corrupt each other, both perish and the lamb will be lost in the infinity of time."

By the end of autumn the gas supply was restored in several districts of the town and the street-cars ran regularly in the main thoroughfares. A new bridge was being built

over the Danube which people were still crossing by motor-
ferry.

With the arrival of the cool weather work started in the
lumberyard as well. Kovács Jr. had to go back from the cable
factory to his old job. By day, haulers carried the wood
away by cart or lorry and by night thieves overran the yard.
To save it from the thieves, the Lumber Co. Ltd. sold off
the entire stock of firewood at one gramme of gold a ton.
Kovács Jr.'s weekly earnings shrank to half.

"You're so thin even a breeze could blow you away,"
Aunty Csics said. "And you've grown ugly, Juli. You'd
better act before he notices it, my girl."

They were sitting in the public bar next to the glowing
iron stove that enveloped the young girl's exhaustion in its
invisible, hot veil. Two cabbies were drinking wine at one
of the corner tables under the naked bulb hanging from the
ceiling that had to be left on all day because of the boarded-up
windows. The water tap gurgled softly and from time to
time dropped a yellow, big-bellied bubble into the sheet-
iron sink.

"He won't wait after tomorrow," the inn-keeper's wife
said with her elbows on the table. "He can have as many
women as he wants."

"Where do we meet?" Juli asked.

"At the Eastern Railway Station, on the departure side."

"In the afternoon?"

"He'll be there at four." The woman lifted up a big
brown parcel onto the table. "There are shoes in it, stock-
ings, warm underwear, a dress and a coat. Put it on, all
of it, because you may have to travel on the roof of the
train."

"But it's impossible tomorrow," the girl whispered desperately, "tomorrow it's Sunday and on Sunday the Cheshire Cat stays at home all day!"

"He won't wait after tomorrow," the inn-keeper's wife said.

Juli dropped her head on the table. "It can't be done on Sunday!"

"Then stay where you are," the woman shrugged. "He won't wait longer."

The two cabbies touched their glasses together.

"I must go home," Juli said from behind her palm. "If he doesn't find me . . ."

"You can both croak together!" the woman nodded. "I've worn myself out running back and forth for your sake, I've been putting off Feri for a week now . . ."

Juli raised her head.

"That's all blah-blah, Aunty Csics. How much are you making on this business?"

"Not enough, my girl," the woman nodded. "Not enough. Less than if I brought up a pig from County Somogy."

" How much?"

"Ten dollars," the inn-keeper's wife said. "If I hand you over to him tomorrow afternoon at the Eastern Railway Station. That's all you are worth, my girl."

Juli bowed her head. One of the cabbies turned back. "What are you crying for, Miss?" he asked. "Have they taken away your fiancé to be a little robot?"

Aunty Csics folded her hands over her stomach. "As far as I'm concerned you do what you want. I told Bellus yesterday that I won't move a finger after this . . . Either you go tomorrow or you stay!"

"Why doesn't he talk to me?... Why is he sending messages?" Juli whispered.

"Do you wonder?" the woman laughed. "Is he going to ask to be thrown out again?'

"Where does he want to take me?"

"To a good place."

Juli hit the table with her fist.

"I asked you where?"

Aunty Csics put her arm round the girl's shoulder. "To a good place, my girl," she repeated quietly. "To the country-side, to Baranya, to fatten you up a bit and let you rest. Then, in two or three weeks, you'll come back to Budapest, move into another district, so you shouldn't run into your bull by accident . . ."

"It's Sunday tomorrow!" the girl cried irritably, "Doesn't he understand that on Sunday it's impossible?"

The cabby turned back again. "Why is it impossible, Miss?" he croaked. "Do you have to go to church? . . . And what is impossible if I may ask? If it is what I am thinking of, Sunday is just as good as any other day."

"What's the matter with you?" asked the inn-keeper's wife looking at the girl attentively. She was staring ahead of her, her face livid, as if the storm raging outside had suddenly moved into her heart and were tearing at the slow-growing, pink buds of her consciousness. Autumn, that a few days ago seemed to have visited the land as a guest only, to wipe away the perspiration on the face of the earth, was raging madly; with its icy breath it tore the roofs from the injured houses, tore the grenade-wounded trees from the side-walk and, snatching the leaves off all the town's trees within an hour made them dance in dense, darkly rustling clouds, above the streets. The rubbish that had collected in the ditches of the suburban streets leaped over the fences and penetrated into the still windowless houses.

"What's the matter?" the inn-keeper's wife repeated.

"'Hell kill me," Juli whispered and a drop of perspiration settled on the side of her pale nose. "I won't get away with it, Aunty Csics! He'll find me and strangle me. I wish I'd never met him."

"Rubbish," the woman murmured.

Juli shook her head. "It's enough for him to take hold of my neck and I am finished. I must tell you I always knew it would end like that!"

"All's well that ends well," the cabby raised his drunken glass to them. "You have nothing to worry about, Miss, while you see me, I've finished off quite a few stinking Jews in my time!"

The inn-keeper's wife burst out laughing. Outside the storm drummed insanely on the tin sign-board of the pub and from the ruined house opposite bricks fell on the side-walk with loud thumps. Suddenly the door of the pub flew open as if it had been pushed in by the wind; a thick cloud of dust rolled along the long bar, then with a loud bang the door closed again. A man stood behind the churning, slowly settling dust wiping his eyes.

"Bellus!" the inn-keeper's wife exclaimed surprised.

Juli drew back in her chair.

"Did you know he was coming?"

"Of course I didn't . . . Bellus, did you tell me that you were coming here?"

The man was still wiping his eyes. "I can't see," he said, "Goddamn it, I can't open my eyes! Why should I tell you?"

"Go away!" Juli cried, "go away!"

The man bent forward a little. "Is that you, Juli?" he asked. "Wait!"

He shook his head and one of his eyes opened. "I'd know your voice among a thousand women . . . Give me some wine and soda, Aunty Csics!"

"Go away!" Juli repeated.

The man broke into a smile and with a quick movement sat down next to the girl. "So you are here," he said calmly. "Did you get the clothes?"

Aunty Csics put her hand on the parcel. "Here they are."

"I can see now," said Bellus. "Put on everything you find there because we may have to travel on the roof of the train."

Juli shook her head. "I am not going away with you."

The chauffeur looked into her eyes. "Let's be at the station at four," he said quietly, "on the departure side, because if the train to Pécs comes in we'll get on it at once."

"I won't be there," Juli said.

The man smoothed down his moustache. "There's no scarf in the parcel, but I'll bring one to the station."

"Don't," Juli said, "because I am not going with you."

Bellus smiled again. "We'll see."

"You won't get your will, not if you crucify yourself," cried the girl pressing both fists to her breast. "And don't you dare send me any more messages or, so help me God, I'll tell István!"

"Why haven't you told him before?"

The girl turned pale. "Because you aren't worth my causing him a single sleepless night, that's why!"

"My little love," the man said in a low voice.

The girl shuddered almost imperceptibly and reclined in her chair. The young man bent forward, took her fists, resting on her breasts, in his hand, twisted them back, pushed his knee between her knees and kissed her on the lips.

"No." Juli whispered, her eyes closed. "No!"

Aunty Csics standing above her laughed hoarsely and a glass overturned on the table. The cabby at the next table rose and tottered towards them his glass raised high.

"Here's to you," he murmured holding on with one hand to Bellus' chair, "God bless all good Magyars! Why aren't you crying now, Miss?"

Outside the storm abated slowly and half an hour later, when Bellus saw the girl home, even the moon emerged now and again between the racing clouds. Above the dark houses whose blind windows did not look back at the moon, a skein of wild geese sailed across the inhuman, windswept sky above Váci Avenue; they came from behind a cloud, like a pendrawing, swam across the moonlight, and a minute later disappeared again behind the fringed mass of fog coming towards them in full flight. The wind howled wildly below them and flung after them all the brilliance of the sky, extinguishing all light on earth. The mud was ankle-deep, only a few empty tins and slivers of glass reflected the heavenly light when the moon drew its veil aside for a second to look down vacantly at the crazy mud.

Reaching the corner of the lumber-yard they stopped. It was so quiet that in between the sharp whistles of the wind they could hear the rustling of the torn posters on the fence of the M. factory opposite. Through the gaping window-holes of the burned-out mill one could look out far upon the Buda mountains.

"Tomorrow at four, then," said Bellus, "on the departure side."

Juli pressed her parcel to her breast.

"Couldn't it be the day after tomorrow?"

"No."

"He doesn't even suspect anything," she said bowing her head, "he doesn't have the remotest idea, it'll hit him like a shot in the belly!"

Bellus made no reply.

"Couldn't we go the day after tomorrow?"

"No," the man said.

Juli raised herself on tip-toe, flung her arms round the man's neck and kissed him on the lips. "At four," she whispered. Her skirt fluttered as she ran towards the fence. Suddenly she stopped, turned back her thin little face and with her moonlit index finger motioned the man to her side.

"Look," she whispered.

At the foot of the fence a large bird cowered in the mud, only its somewhat lighter head and big flat back emerging from the darkness.

"A wild goose," Bellus whispered hoarsely. At the squelching of the mud the bird moved, took a running leap with its wings outstretched, then, with heavy flaps, flew up on the fence. In one jump Bellus reached the fence and, soundlessly like a cat, leaped into the air. He caught the bird as it was about to take off again by the wing.

Juli pressed her hand to her mouth. "Jesus," she sighed. The brown eyes of the wild goose stared into hers and its beak opened soundlessly.

Bellus laughed, then he pressed the squirming bird between

his knees, clasped its neck in his fingers and twisted. The wings stretched out once more, quivering.

"That'll do for a last supper," the man said. "Let him have his fill from your cooking once more."

Juli followed him with her eyes until his wiry figure, his hair fluttering in the wind, disappeared in the shadow of the mill. Twenty feet further on the wood-thieves breaking into the yard had torn a hole in the fence; Juli slipped in through the opening, hid the parcel among the boards in one stack, then set out running towards the office. Kovács Jr. was lying on the straw mattress under the kerosene lamp that swung on a nail in the wall, sleeping. He breathed regularly, his face was as smooth as an infant's, his right hand rested on his huge, concave belly. He must have been very tired because he bore the parting glance lying heavy on his face with the rhythm of his breathing unchanged and woke only when the girl turned her face suddenly away. He sat up, smiled at Juli and held out his arms to her.

"I fell asleep," he grumbled bashfully. "Give me something to eat. What's that in your hand?"

"Why don't you cover up when you lie down!" Juli said. "How often do I have to tell you, you can catch cold lying down!"

"I'm not cold," the giant shook his head. "What's that you've got?"

"A foreign goose."

Kovács Jr. fingered it. "It's still warm, poor thing," he said. "I saw them fly over this afternoon. The storm must have knocked it down. Will you cook it?"

Juli squatted down by the stove and with a flat piece of wood cleaned out the ashes. "Lie down again, Cheshire

Cat," she said, "It'll be a long time before supper is ready."

"Don't you want to talk to me?" the giant asked sadly.

The girl kept her back to him, her face invisible. "Of course, I do," she said. "I thought you were tired."

"When you are with me I am never tired," the giant said in a surprised voice, "but when you go away from me I want nothing but sleep. You are like the air to me."

"Shut up!" Juli cried. "Lie down and sleep!"

Kovács Jr. burst out laughing. "*Ne moj jos da mi sferes postelju, mamice,*" he said quietly.

Juli turned back. "What are you jabbering?"

"That was in Serbian," Kovács Jr. explained. "It means: don't put me to bed yet, mummy! Back home, at Barcs, when I used to come home off the hillside, my mother used to feed me and bed me down straight off at the foot of her bed. That's what I used to tell her."

"And now you are crying," Juli said turning away from him.

"I always do when I think of my mother," Kovács Jr. shook his head. "I'm not exactly crying, but my eyes fill with tears . . . I've told you about that."

"When?"

"Have you forgotten already?" the giant asked unbelievingly. "When I first met you in front of No. 17 Teréz Avenue. I've never forgotten a single word you said since."

The fire flared up in the stove and ran up the girl's shadow on the wall which, with a large movement like a cenophare on Athene's temple, raised the large shadow of a pot above its head.

"Hush, good dog!" Juli said. "Lie down and sleep."

Kovács Jr. shook his head. "But I want to talk," he grumbled.

"Well, talk," Juli shrugged her shoulders.

"I haven't forgotten a single letter of anything you said in my hearing these last seven months," Kovács Jr. said happily. "If you died now, I could talk to my heart about you for a whole month."

"If I died?"

The giant jumped up from the straw mattress and with two long strides reached the girl. He grasped her shoulder, patted her arm, her breast, and stroked her hair with his fingers. "Be quiet!" he whispered frightened and clasped his hands entreatingly. "You won't die, Juli. You can't die as long as I'm alive!"

The girl turned suddenly to face him.

"Why not, you idiot?" she shouted flushing with anger.

The giant pressed his palm on his mouth. "Be quiet!" he whispered. "What would happen to me if you died, Juli? I'd be lost in this great big world like a speck of dust!"

"The hell you would!" the girl cried. "Some speck of dust!"

The water in the pot began to boil and quietly translated into its own humming language the turbulent message of the fire working beneath it. Kovács Jr. shook himself and lay back on the mattress. The moon shone through the window on his face.

"You know, Juli," he said quietly, "you are with me exactly as that bright moon up there is with the earth."

"What do you mean?" the girl asked.

The giant laughed happily.

"You can never leave me," he informed her. "You can't help illuminating my heart."

"That's true," said Juli.

The giant went on laughing. "No one has ever left me

except those who died. And no one has ever betrayed me since I first saw the daylight, neither meat-eating, nor plant-eating humans. You'll have it good, Juli, once this great poverty has left us."

"When will that be?"

"When it leaves the others as well," the giant said happily. "Or perhaps a little before that because I am stronger than they are."

Juli made no reply. Outside the storm had almost completely blown itself out, the clouds moved away from above the town and the yellow autumn moon gazed down musingly on the war-torn earth like the eye of a giant wild goose that cannot part from its fatherland and has built its nest in the branches of Nothing to meditate. The Buda mountains glanced with their light-drenched heads across the Danube and examined the moonlit dome of the cathedral. At times a gust of wind churned up the quickly drying dust and fallen leaves outside the window and, like messages beamed to the earth, made the tiny, thick swirls jump over the bright roof of the office building and the tall fence.

"I know that you wanted to leave me," the giant said.

Juli turned slowly back and faced Kovács Jr.

"What did you say?" she asked, blenching.

The giant nodded.

"When we had that dinner party, that's when you wanted to leave me."

"It isn't true," the girl stammered.

"Ha-ha-ha," Kovács Jr. laughed. "I scared you so much, that time, that you wanted to leave me. I knew that if I put just one finger on Mr. Bellus you would fly away in fear the next day, or the day after, like a bird."

"It isn't true," Juli cried, "It isn't true!"

The giant shook his head. "What did you tell me when you found me at the other end of the yard?"

"How should I know?"

"You said: sweet Cheshire Cat, my only love, I don't want to betray you!"

"So what!" Juli cried and her face turned livid with anger.

"Ha-ha-ha," the giant laughed, "ha-ha-ha! You said that you didn't want to betray me because in your heart you did want to betray me. That's why I cried that time the way I had never cried since my mother's death."

"It's a lie," Juli shouted beside herself with rage, "It's a lie!"

"And what else did you say?" Kovács Jr. asked. "Shall I repeat word for word what you said then?"

The girl ran over to the straw mattress and, bending over the giant held both her tiny fists under his snub-nose. "Shut up," she whispered, "or I'll kill you!"

"You said," the giant went on and beads of perspiration appeared on his frowning forehead, "you said, word for word: I've never loved anyone the way I love you, Cheshire Cat, don't leave me! It isn't my fault if men like me and I too . . ."

He fell silent and wiped away the perspiration running down his temples with the back of his hand. "It isn't my fault if men like me and I too . . ."

"Don't you know the rest?" the girl murmured.

The giant's small blue eyes looked straight into hers.

"You didn't say any more," he growled. "You threw yourself on me and wept. Then you said: carry me home . . . don't touch me there because it hurts, I bruised myself when I fainted . . . Oh, oh . . ."

"Is that all?"

"At home you said: put me down on the bed and lie next to me! ... I love only you in this great big world!"

The girl looked down on the huge pink face of the reclining giant, her eyes flashing with fury. "That's all I said all night long, isn't it?"

The giant sat up and turned his perspiring face towards the girl.

"Hit me, Juli," he said quietly. The girl retreated startled.

"No," she cried wildly, "no!"

"Are you afraid?"

"Shut up!"

"Are you afraid to hit me?" the giant asked sadly.

The girl's teeth were chattering.

"Shut up!"

"If you are afraid to hit me," the giant said, "then you are going to betray me tomorrow, Juli."

"Shut up!" the girl whispered for the third time. She put her arms round the giant's neck, closed her eyes, and trembling in her entire body, kissed him on the mouth. But he did not kiss her back.

"What's the matter with you, Cheshire Cat?" the girl asked drawing back. "Lord, the water is boiling over!"

Kovács Jr. rose, stepped across to the stove and lifted off the sizzling pot. He pulled the wild goose out of the bubbling water by one protuding leg, tore it in two, threw one half back into the pot and bit into the other. "It's hot!" he hissed licking his mouth and began to swing the steaming, dripping flesh by the bone. "Tomorrow afternoon," he said with his head bent, continuing to swing the meat, "tomorrow afternoon we'll go and look at the new bridge they are building, you hear me, Juli? And in the evening we're going to the cinema."

"To the cinema?" the girl asked.

"I was given two tickets," the giant informed her. "We've never been to the cinema together, Juli! I've only been once in my life and then alone."

By the time Kovács Jr. returned next day, Sunday, from his tour of inspection of the office building, Juli was no longer there.

Towards noon, shortly before he set out from home to walk round the lumber yard it had begun to rain. As he did not like getting his long fair hair wet, he covered his head with Juli's one and only pot that sat on his mighty skull like the helmet on Hector's when he went to his death.

"What do you want me to use for cooking?" the girl asked irritably. The giant laughed and went out into the rain.

In a remote corner of the lumber yard, near the Danube, three men and a small woman were stealing wood. The giant stopped short behind one of the stacks and, pressing his hand to his heart, with the rain-splashed pot on his head, stood silently watching the handcart loaded with timber and the drenched men working hurriedly and soundlessly around it. The tiny old woman worked separately, on her own account: she was gathering trimmings in a rucksack and two shopping bags; enough to warm her poor old back and a plate of soup. If she could come out every day, perhaps she would survive the winter, the giant thought; but for whose sake would you survive, mother? The sky was completely covered by the leaden autumnal blanket of cloud, not a single chink of hope showed in it.

One of the men stood on top of the wood stack, lifting the boards by one end and sliding them obliquely down on to the ground where the other two tipped them on the hand-cart. At this end of the yard 25–30 wagonloads of timber still stood stacked up in undisturbed order and behind it a few wagonloads of fire-wood, beech and hornbeam brought up the Danube on floats during the war. The gate at the river end was opened only when a ship had to be unloaded; deliveries were made through the northern gate opening on N. Street, and thus, naturally, the wood stacked up here was the last to be touched. The narrow little streets between the stacks were overgrown with weed.

"Who are you?" asked one of the men turning round.

The young lad standing on top of the pyre flung down the log he was holding.

"He must be the guard."

"Sure thing."

"What are you waiting for?" the other man called up, "slide that board down!"

The heavy board creaked and fell with a thud. The three men worked on turning their backs on Kovács Jr. Further away the little old woman was squatting on the ground filling her rucksack. The rain pattered gently down on the boards.

"Are you still there?" asked the lad on top of the stack after a while. "What are you staring at? Have you nothing better to do than to stand around in the rain?"

"Go home, old man," the other men said from beside the cart, "go home to your dinner."

Kovács Jr. wiped the rainwater from his face with the back of his hand. From the sudden movement the pot tilted a little forward and slipped down on his forehead.

"Stop it," he said. "That wood doesn't belong to you."

"Is it yours perhaps?"

Kovács Jr. made no reply.

"Is it yours?" one of the older men asked again, "tell me, is it yours?"

The old woman straightened up from her squatting position and padded towards them. Kovács Jr. shook his head.

"He's showing us it isn't his," the lad on top of the stack said mockingly. "In that case what the hell do you want from us?"

The giant raised his hand.

"I'll help you to unload the cart," he said.

"What does he say?" one of the men asked in surprise.

"I'll help you to unload," Kovács Jr. repeated. The man stared silently into his face, then turned away and went back to his cart. "Go to hell!" he said.

In the meantime the tiny old woman reached Kovács Jr.'s side and stretched out her neck attentively to examine the red enamelled pot on the giant's head. "Is it whole?" she asked, "tell me, son, is it whole?"

Kovács Jr. reached up and patted the pot. "It is," he said.

"I have a perfectly new hat at home from a good shop in town," the old woman informed him, "you can have in exchange if it is really whole. It's absolutely new, son, I brought it from the shop myself three days after the Russians came in."

The two men lifted another board on to the cart. Kovács Jr. pushed the tiny old woman aside with one hand and with the other again wiped away the rainwater that ran into his eyes. "What do you want from them?" the little old woman screeched in sudden anger, "Leave them alone! Is that wood yours?"

The giant shook his head. "It isn't mine, aunty, I'm only guarding it."

"Who are you guarding it for?" the old woman asked indignantly. "For the Germans?"

Kovács Jr. looked up to the top of the stack. "How do you mean, for the Germans?"

"Well, how should I know for whom?" the old woman grumbled. "Whether it is for the Swabians, or the Jews, or what do I know? Or for the house-owners in the city! Why don't they guard it themselves? They make a watchdog of you, God send them to hell for depriving us of just a little warmth before we're laid in the ground!"

Another board slid down from the top of the stack and hit the ground. The giant took the pot from his head. "Stop that!" he cried, "that wood is not yours!"

"You go to hell," panted the older man over the board that whipped up and down on his shoulder. "I told you to go to hell!" The other man drew a gun from his pocket. "Didn't you hear him?"

The giant made no reply.

"About turn!"

The rain which had stopped completely for a few minutes came down again, rapping on the boards and laying its nervous whip across the necks of the soaked men. "Are you still here?" said the man with the gun.

The giant slapped the water from his face.

"That wood doesn't belong to you!" he repeated quietly and his lips whitened, "because you haven't worked for it."

"Idiot!" the older man murmured. The other man's

face twitched. "Tell him to get to hell out of here or I won't
answer for myself," he said swearing. The old woman gave
a frightened scream and pressed her hands to her lips. "Tell
him to go away or I'll shoot him in the belly!" the man
with the gun said and his face twitched again. The giant
took a step forward. The gun, going off immediately, hit
him in the arm but he never noticed, all he heard was a
short, sharp crack. He shook his head, then turned on his
heel and, without looking back, set out homewards. On the
way, blood began to drip from under his sleeve, once or twice
he licked it off his palm but as it wouldn't stop and his hand
became stickier and stickier, he took his jacket off and
examined the wound. The bullet had only grazed his arm.

Juli was not in the room. Kovács Jr. went out of the
house, looked around the landscape cut into sections by
curtains of rain, then returned to the room. He washed out
his wound in the basin and then sat down on the straw
mattress to rest. Time passed slowly. In order to hurry it on
he made up the fire towards noon and, as lonely people are
wont to do, conversed in thought with the more friendly
objects in his entourage. But by the time he was ready to
put the water on to boil he noticed that he had lost the pot.
Whether he had taken it off at the scene of the robbery or on
the way home, when he examined his wound, he could no
longer remember. He patted his head: his hair was soaking
wet. Outside, however, the rain had slowed so he set out to
find the pot.

The wood thieves had vanished but there wasn't a trace of
the pot either at the scene of the shooting or on the way. He
looked around carefully but the pot remained as undiscover-
able as Juli. He called loudly for one, obviously so that the

other should hear. "Pot, my little pot, where have you gone?" he cried forming his palms into a trumpet lest the words dissolve in the rain-soaked, silent landscape. But only hopelessness replied to the melodious question with its muted notes.

For two days he didn't move from the lumber yard and during that time he neither ate nor drank. On the third day he rose early and set out to find the girl. He went straight to the new building; that's what they had planned to visit together before Juli left him and it was not impossible that— should she want to return to him but be ashamed to show up at the lumber yard—she should end up here in her unhappy wanderings.

Along the Váci Avenue and St. István Boulevard they had already walked together. "Will you buy me a cream puff?" Juli had asked outside a pastry shop. She stood before the shop window, her legs spread, her neck stretched forward, and prodded the glass with her pointed forefinger. "You've no money?" she cried amazed, "heavens, how come you've no money? Where did you put it?... into the bank? Or have you spent it again on women and champagne? Shame on you!"

She turned back twice for a look at the cream puff with an enchanting expression of yearning, tilting her head a little to the side, her red lips parted, her dark eyes flashing with emotion, then she spat out angrily and quickened her steps. "Why don't they elect you king," she said linking her arm into Kovács Jr.'s, "aren't you the strongest man in the country? Gosh, I'd stuff myself so full of cream puffs that I'd simply kick the bucket with delight! And you'd be so unhappy that you would hang yourself on the spire of the

Mátyás church with the gold crown on your head . . . What are you stopping for, Cheshire Cat? Don't drool, everyone doesn't have to see how happy you are!"

At one of the houses he stopped short.

"This is where I lived for a year long ago, when I was a young lady," she said clicking her tongue. "It was a first-class flat with all the comforts, there was even an embroidered blessing on the wall. What did I do afterwards? I sold holy pictures in the countryside."

Her mobile face darkened, her nostrils flared, a shadowy spot appeared on her temples. "Come on," she said pinching Kovács Jr.'s sleeve between two fingers and pulling him away impatiently, "why are you standing about on the street corner? That isn't elegant at all! Once we're friends, I'll tell you what happened to me in this house. You want me to tell you now? Not in the street! . . . Shall I whisper it? . . . Bend down . . . Lower . . . No, I won't tell you after all, it embarrasses me. If you buy me a cream puff I'll write it down for you in a letter. Move your ear, will you?"

"Sweet Cheshire Cat," she said after a little while in front of a crooked advertising pillar, opposite the wreck of the Margaret Bridge; the river made tiny, frothing swirls round its sunken iron girders. "Sweet Cheshire Cat, you don't even know that you saved me. I shall never leave you!"

As he turned into Személynök Street his memory fell silent. The street was so deserted that the giant gasped for breath. Had he taken hold of himself he could have continued the half-orphan conversation even in this environment where the girl had never walked and which suddenly belched up all the empty darkness, but he had no strength left. He began to run. From the direction of the new bridge building site one could already distinguish the high whine of the electric drills.

He loafed around until late in the evening near the fence surrounding the bridge-head. He would have stayed there all night had he not feared that the girl might return to the lumber yard in the meantime and, not finding him there to hold her back, run off again. He got home by midnight and at dawn set out again. He did not return to the bridge, however, because he couldn't have faced the disappointment.

He roamed the town for three weeks, mostly along the streets where he and Juli walked together. He never returned to any of them a second time, because from every doorway the girl's absence glared back at him with insane eyes as if it wanted to entice him into the bridal bed of oblivion. At the corner of Dohány Street where once her voice had sounded, now only the silence screamed. In the Lehel market the cabbages yearned for her non-existent hand. On the sandy Danube shore, where on hot summer evenings she had swum naked, the water retreated before her imagined foot and washed around her quickly materializing white hips. When the wind blew along Váci Avenue each fluttering skirt flapped around her knees. At night, in the dark street, each breath coming towards him accosted the giant.

As the owner of the lumber yard had hired a new guard, Kovács Jr. moved his blanket, his shirt and his red pot that had turned up again in the meantime, into Uncle Csipesz's place. The old man asked nothing, but at night when his guest came home he rose from his bed, made up the fire in the small, round iron stove, warmed up a little soup or mash and fed the giant. The ancient man was so thin that Kovács Jr. could lie on his back on the straw mattress as if he were lying next to a line. Uncle Csipesz's eighty years made do with five or six hours of sleep, it was out of politeness more than anything else that he lay down again on the bed so as not to scare away his now homeless former landlord. In the morning they rose at the same time, the old man knelt down in the corner to pray and Kovács Jr. went into town.

On one occasion, loafing around Calvin Square he came face to face with Aunty Csics, the inn-keeper's wife. He didn't recognize her right away and the woman walked by quickly. But after ten steps she felt the panting breath of the giant on her neck and frightened she turned to face him.

"What do you want?" she asked, her lips trembling.

"I didn't recognize you," the giant said, "my eyes are tired because I cry a great deal nowadays."

The woman grew calmer.

"Why do you cry?"

Kovács Jr. bent his head.

"Juli is lost," he said.

"What do you mean, she is lost?" the woman asked amazed.

"She left home two weeks ago and she hasn't come back," muttered the giant. "Something must have happened to her that she can't come home."

"Have you reported it to the police?"

"Not yet," the giant shook his head, "not yet! The police couldn't help me, Aunty Csics! Haven't you seen her?"

The woman retreated a step or two.

"Not me, Mr. Kovács," she said.

"Then what is to be done?" the giant asked, covering his face with his huge palms to hide his flush. "I've been walking the town for two weeks, but I've tired my eyes in vain, I can't find any trace of her. Won't you help me?"

"Gladly," the woman said. "How could I help, Mr. Kovács?"

They walked side by side silently, the giant made no reply. Before the burned-out ruins of a house on the corner of Kecskeméti Street he stopped suddenly and carefully examined the bleak, filthy walls.

"It's like my heart," he said quietly after a while, "broken and filthy. Would you help me, Aunty Csics?"

"Gladly," the woman repeated, "gladly. But how, Mr. Kovács?"

The giant raised his head and looked into the woman's eyes.

"Where is Juli?"

"How should I know that, my dear, good Mr. Kovács?" the woman cried blenching. "I'd have told you long ago if I knew!"

"You don't know?" the giant shook his head, "you don't know? Of course, you know. You don't tell me because you are afraid of me."

"The Lord strike me dead if I know!" the inn-keeper's wife cried. "What gives you the idea that it was me?"

The giant clasped the woman's wrist in his fingers.

"If I think back now," he said, "it seems to me that it was when you began to visit us at the lumber yard that Juli started to change."

"Let go of my hand!" the woman hissed. The giant relaxed his fingers immediately and stepped back.

"Of course I let you go," he murmured. "I don't want to hurt you! But since you began to come out in the afternoons, Juli changed completely. She no longer sang and when I looked into her eyes, she squinted. Do tell me where she is!"

"What do you want from me?" the woman whispered and her voice became furry with fear. "Leave me alone!"

"What was it you told me when we had that dinner party last summer? What did you say about women? Wait a minute, I can remember it exactly." He fell silent, bowed his head, deep parallel furrows appeared on his forehead from between which shining drops of perspiration descended a moment later to the corners of his nose and along both temples. "I was standing in front of the house watching the guests around the fire and I was happy that I could feed you. After a while you all came up to me, surrounded me, and a red-haired woman with a small black cat in her arms, I'd never met her before, said ... Don't you remember, Aunty Csics, what she said?"

"I don't remember," the inn-keeper's wife replied. "I'm busy now, Mr. Kovács, why don't you come to the shop tomorrow?"

"And you don't remember what you said either?"

"Let go of my hand!" the woman screamed.

Again the giant released her wrist. "You said," he continued his head bowed, wiping away the acid perspiration that ran into his eyes from his face, "you said that every woman could be seduced. That every woman could be seduced, but one has to know the way. Was that what you said, Aunty Csics?"

"Let go of my hand," the woman hissed for the third time.

For the third time the giant released her. "You also said that there wasn't a woman who couldn't be bought for a kilo of flour. And that every woman had her price. Is that what you said, Aunty Csics?"

"What do I know what I said," the woman growled. "If you don't let me go I'll shout for help!"

"And how did it happen," the giant asked shaking his head slowly, "that since you began visiting us at the yard we ate white bread and bacon more than once and Juli got into the habit of smoking cigarettes?"

The inn-keeper's wife tore her hand from the giant's fingers. "What do I care about your bacon!" she cried her face flushed with fear. Several passers-by turned back, a man pulling a hand-cart stopped by the ravaged side-walk and, dropping the pole of the cart looked closely at the motionless giant staring ahead of him his head bent. The woman turned away suddenly and, crossing the square, set out hurriedly towards Museum Street. Kovács Jr. followed her with his eyes for a while, then he walked along Kecskeméti Street, out to the Danube.

Towards the end of the third week he found himself at the scene of their first meeting, in front of No. 17 Teréz Avenue. He sat on the sidewalk for two whole days, leaning against the house wall. On the afternoon of the second day, just before dusk fell, he caught sight of Juli.

She was walking on the other side of the Avenue in the direction of the Western Railway Station. She wore an overcoat, she had new shoes on her feet, a dark-red scarf on her head, tied under the chin and she carried a short-handled black umbrella. The giant recognized her by her gait, that delightful half-town, half-country way of walking. She strode forward, holding herself erect like the peasant girls, but walking with soft, springy steps befitting the pavements. He would have known her among a thousand women by her carriage.

He stumbled to his feet and looked himself up and down: his trousers were torn and muddy, his hands dirty, his toes stuck out from both his shoes. He wiped his hands in his trousers so as not to soil Juli's new clothes, bent back his toes so they shouldn't show through the crack, smoothed his hair down with his palm, his face and forehead with the sleeve of his jacket, then he ran after the girl. He had no idea what he would do with her.

He crossed the street and was almost hit by a car. He elbowed the passers-by out of his way; a woman fell but he did not help her to her feet. He did not hear the shouts behind him. Reaching the other side-walk he stopped and, growling loudly, pressed his hand to his heart. The girl was not alone; a man was walking at her side.

He too was well dressed, like Juli; he wore a black hat, a long overcoat and a silk scarf round his neck. He had grey, knitted gloves on his hands and he limped a bit with his left leg. Juli was just taking his arm, with that same, unforgettable movement with which, at the dawn of their love, she used to take Kovács Jr.'s; as if her tiny hands were seeking refuge and, at the same time, guarding her possession. She laid her fingers on the inside of the man's elbow. The giant stopped and turned away his head.

By the time he set out after them again they had disappeared in the thickening crowd in front of the railway station. He found them again on Váci Street two or three minutes later: they stood in a doorway, facing each other and talking. Juli had her back towards the giant. By the time he reached them they were just about to enter the door. The man's face blurred before his eyes, the giant saw only that he had a moustache.

"Can we help you?" the man asked. The girl turned back. She had a tiny wart on her left nostril; it was not Juli. The giant pressed his hand to his heart and stepped back.

"What do you want?" the man asked impatiently.

He received no answer. The giant stood there for another second then he turned about and set out homewards.

In Uncle Csipesz's room a stranger was sitting at the table pouring wine from a bottle into a glass. The old man squatted on his mattress drawing the blanket over his shivering shoulders. When the giant pushed in the door he jumped up surprised.

"He doesn't usually come home so early." he said in his deep bass voice turning to the stranger. "But lo, on the Day of Armageddon the accused arrive on time to receive their sentence."

The stranger had a letter from Juli for the giant. It was dated three weeks back, just before her death. On their way to Pécs, just outside Dombovár, she and Bellus had been swept off the roof of the train by a low tunnel entrance. The man was killed on the spot, Juli was carried, her bones broken, to a signalman's house where she lived for another two days. She had written the letter on a page torn from a copy book, a few hours before she died. She had scribbled only two lines on the paper in her childish hand: "Sweet Cheshire Cat," the letter said, "forgive me for having betrayed you. Forget me because I am now going to die."

Having no place to sleep, the signalman spent the night with Uncle Csipesz; it was probably for this reason he had brought the letter. He had flour and smoked meat from the countryside to sell in Budapest. Uncle Csipesz and he slept on the mattress, the giant spent the night sitting at the table, awake.

At dawn the old man woke the stranger.

"Were you there when the little Miss died?" he asked bending over the bed. His long white beard hung down vertically on the blanket.

"Yes," the man said. "We even accompanied her to the churchyard, my son and I. I can show you her grave, if you want me to."

"Are you sure you got her name right?" Uncle Csipesz asked.

The signalman pushed the old man's beard aside and climbed out of bed. "Juli Szandál" he said. "She wrote it down on the back of the letter in case I forgot . . . Look, where does this Mrs. Csics, live? They told me she would buy my flour."

"Who said so?"

"Juli Szandál," the signalman grunted pulling on his boots with a deep sigh. "She said to bring her letter because that woman lived near here and was sure to buy my flour."

The old man prodded the railwayman's chest with his pointed index finger.

"I'll lead you to her, Mister," he said. "Will you give me a little piece of sausage for it? No larger than my beard."

Outside the November wind blew roaring and flung the pouring rain in thick sheaves against the window. A dense, yellowish fog rolled up from the Danube in the narrow streets between the wood piles. Two shots were heard in the distance.

"Did the little Miss suffer much?" the old man asked holding on to his beard and bending forward curiously. "When did she give up her soul? During the day or at night? Those of clean heart always die at night, son."

Without waiting for an answer he turned round and went up to the giant sitting at the table.

"Let's sing the little Miss's favourite song, Mr. Kovács," he said, "the one you were wont to sing together. I know only the first words, it begins:

Hajaja bugaci Postume, Postume!"

The giant rose.

"God be with you, Uncle," he said putting his hand on the old man's shoulder. "Thank you for your kind hospitality. May you remain in good health."

"Where are you going?" the old man asked. "Couldn't I come with you, Mr. Kovács?"

The giant shook his head.

"I'm going home to Barcs, to the lumber yard," he said. "They promised me they'd take me back if I grew tired of this big town. I shall work in the woods, Uncle. In ten years I'll come back here, but by then I won't find you alive, Uncle."

# BEHIND THE BRICK WALL

# BEHIND THE BRICK WALL

Comrade Bodi left Karoly Brock Street, which led to the main gate of the factory, turned into the first side street, and a few minutes later came out onto the bank of the Danube. He still had half an hour until the relief of the night shift. He had time to take a stroll and enjoy the early spring sunshine. He had a headache.

Across the Danube, in Pest, he could see the long row of dust-coloured warehouses and, farther off, the bridge, above which seagulls slowly wheeled. The wind blew strongly from the west, ruffling the river and chasing the garbage along the water's edge. When the gusts became more violent, yellow clouds of dust suddenly rose into the air, darkening the sun. The river's edge, left derelict, was littered with rubbish. Some way off, beside the water, a stray dog, shaggy and emaciated, sniffed at some dried-up filth and watched uneasily as the man approached.

There the high, red brick wall which surrounded the factory broke the force of the wind a little. Garbage strewed the ground beneath the wall, but at least a man's eyes and mouth were not filled with grit and sand when the wind blew too hard. Comrade Bodi stopped a moment, his back to the wind. He leaned against the wall, turning to the sun his thin face with its day's growth of beard. Just as he was about to set off again, he noticed a brand-new piece of leather at his feet, partly covered with sand brought by the last gust of wind. It was twelve or fifteen inches long. Comrade Bodi picked it up, studied it carefully, then went on his way with the thick piece of leather in his hand.

He had hardly gone a few steps when another piece of strap fell in front of him, almost grazing his cap, and coming from the other side of the brick wall. A third and fourth followed, curving in a great arc over the wall. Comrade Bodi examined them for a few moments and then continued on his way. On the other side of the wall there was a low storeroom attached to the workshops.

Bodi made his way straight to the locker room. Every morning he slipped on a pair of oil-stained overalls to save his clothes.

"What's this?" asked a machinist, sitting on a bench near by.

"What?"

The man had pulled off his shoe. His big toe, yellow and crooked, poked through a hole in his sock. Carefully, he removed the sock and held it up between two fingers.

"What's this?"

Comrade Bodi averted his head slightly. "Are you talking to me?" he asked.

"Yes, what's this?" the worker repeated, waving the sock in front of Bodi's face.

Bodi turned his head even more. "Take it away," he said quietly.

"Don't you know what it is?" asked the worker. "It's the 'sock of the new Man'."

The night shift was already leaving. Some of the workers greeted Bodi. Others did not. Some had known Bodi for twenty years, ever since he had come to the factory, yet they passed without a word. Bodi went across the yard, where the wind lashed at his face once more. Here the air seemed denser, more solid, because of the litter suspended in it. In another part of the plant, employees arrived one by one at the main office. Comrade Bodi reached the office in his turn.

Behind the desk sat a corpulent man with a face marked by illness, flesh yellow and puffy beneath the eyes, jowls flabby and wrinkled. Bodi greeted him. The man nodded curtly, then asked, "What's wrong now?"

"They're stealing the leather now."

The fat man said nothing.

"I saw it with my own eyes."

"Where?"

"Shop Number Four," said Bodi. "They're throwing the belting over the wall. I was walking at the back of the factory."

The two men stared at each other without speaking.

"Makes leather to mend their shoes," said the fat man, the corners of his mouth twisted in a faintly sarcastic grimace.

An old man wearing eyeglasses, tall and stooping, came into the office. He gave a humble greeting and then, as if expecting a kick in the ass, fled precipitately into the next room. Two workers followed him; one, a slight girl with dimples, had a face as fresh as the peonies she had been picking that morning in her garden before leaving for the plant. Comrade Bodi waited until the door was shut, then rested his hand on the desk. The flesh of the hand was blue-white, the nails trimmed close.

"It can't go on like this," he said. "No, not like this. God! Not any more."

"I'll see about it," said the fat man. He spoke with a tired air, staring vacantly at the door through which the peony-girl had disappeared.

Outside again, Bodi had the wind behind him. An empty oil drum began to roll before the force of the wind; it clanged to a stop against the wall of the gasoline depot. The wind was fresh, a fine spring wind. The workshop windows set up such a rattling that he could hardly make out the din of the mechanical hammers.

In the workshop, someone was waiting for Bodi. He worked in a corner of the assembly shop, in a glassed-in cubicle through the door of which so much soot and dust blew that at night the shift had coal-black faces and hair gritty with metal dust. The place was full of people waiting or jostling. The foreman stood by the window, lost in some document, his glasses pushed up onto his forehead. The man waiting for Bodi stood with his head bent; he slouched against the wall and did not look up until Bodi took his place behind the desk.

"Hello, Ferenc," said Bodi.

The man took a step forward.

"What's up?"

"Do you know what's going on?"

Comrade Bodi looked at the production schedule the man held out to him.

"You know," the man went on. "You're responsible. What the hell does it mean?"

Comrade Bodi examined the sheet more closely. "Don't get excited, Ferenc," he said.

The paper continued to shake.

"Where do you get this crap?" the man went on, speaking in a low, desperate voice. "Ninety seconds per piece! What kind of a norm is that? You want me to live on love?"

"Don't get excited, Ferenc."

The man put the paper on the desk. "Where do you get a crazy norm like this?" he said, his voice still low. "Just tell me how. If you can show me how, all right. I'll go back to my bench. But show me."

"In the morning, from now on," Bodi said, "you won't have to wait until the materials arrive. You gain half an hour from that alone."

"You think so?" said the man, ironically. "What next?"

Bodi avoided his eyes. "You know it's necessary, Ferenc," he said. "Production costs are too high. We're eating into reserves. Expenses are so heavy that . . ."

"Is that so?"

Bodi looked at him out of the corner of his eye, to see if he was being sarcastic. "That is so," he replied. "Don't be funny."

"Funny?" said the man.

There was silence. Comrade Bodi turned to the door which had opened; no doubt it was a visitor for him. He folded the paper on the desk.

"How much do I take home?" the man said. "Don't give me that paper back. Work it out. See what I get deducted. See what I'll take home to the wife and kids. Work it out!"

"Put your back into it, Ferenc," said Bodi. "You'll make it up in a month." He got no reply; he raised his eyes. Ferenc was looking him in the eyes for the first time since the beginning of the interview. Comrade Bodi turned away his head. The man turned on his heels and left the cubicle without a word.

"There's a man who hasn't got any love for you," said the typist near Bodi.

A few minutes later Bodi walked through the workshop

again—the manager had just sent for him—and noticed that Ferenc's bench was empty. The violent wind snatched the workshop door from his grasp and sailed his cap toward a puddle of oily water that had lain in a hollow of the clay-like soil since last week's rain. Two young apprentices sniggered when they saw the cap blowing along toward the puddle. A third, coming toward Bodi, could have put out his foot to stop it, but seeing Bodi running he looked the other way. The two apprentices guffawed. The cap fell in the greasy water. Bodi shook it out and went on slowly. He felt their eyes on his back.

On his way from the manager's office he skirted the administration building. Behind the metal shop, in a narrow alleyway between the red brick wall and the workshop, he let himself slowly down to the ground, his back against the wall. No one ever came here. His head was splitting. The world seemed dark around him. His eyes throbbed, misted over with tears of pain. His forehead ran with sweat.

Usually these attacks came in the evening, between eight and ten o'clock. Sometimes he suffered during the day, but the worst pains did not come until evening, at supper or after. For two years now he had not gone out after work nor after his evening meal, except on the days when he had a Party meeting. On Sundays he stayed in bed; on that day the pain never left him. He tried all kinds of analgesics: aspirin, pills, sedatives—the whole range of cures. What helped most was to lie down with his head hanging off the bed.

Here, beyond the workshop where no one came, he told himself he could rest for just a quarter of an hour. He stretched himself at full length. He was at the foot of the wall, sheltered from the wind which crept into the alley, sometimes raising dense clouds of dust. He rested his neck on a brick and tilted his head backward. Above him long, boat-shaped clouds sped so quickly across the blue sky that they made him dizzy. "I'll shut my eyes," he said to himself. As he shut his eyes, the wind whistled in his ears. Go back again to the doctor? What for? For two years he had trailed from one hospital to another. At first the doctors had suspected a tumor on the brain: they examined the back of his eyes, X-rayed his skull and brain. Then they had sent him to a nerve specialist. Then to the general section. Six months before, they had done a cisternal puncture. "Undress and don't worry. I am going to insert a needle in the nape of your neck. It won't hurt. Don't move, or the prick could cause a fatal lesion. It will only hurt for a moment. Don't be afraid. Be calm." He had not felt much pain, but when the thick needle had plunged into his neck he had felt something he would never forget. It was worse than anything until then.

Back in the cubicle the foreman asked: "What did the old man want?" He pushed his glasses back on his forehead.

Bodi shrugged.

"Production costs?"

"He talked about that."

"What else?"

"The thefts."

"Our fault, I suppose?"

"Well," said Bodi, "I'm a member of the council for discipline."

"That's a big leg up."

"He's right," Bodi said. "I'm not active enough. I lack vigilance, enthusiasm. He's right."

8                                   T.G.

"You think so?"

"Yes," said Bodi. "I think he's right."

"What are you shutting your eyes for?" asked the foreman. "Are you sick? What's the matter?"

"Nothing's wrong. Nothing at all."

The foreman stepped toward Bodi. "You look like a corpse."

Comrade Bodi began to laugh. "No, I'm fine. By the way, yesterday was Karcsi Olajos' trial."

"The fool! What did he get?"

"Six months."

The foreman looked at Bodi without a word. His round Magyar face, with its little stiff moustache, had gone white with rage.

"That's a hell of a story to take around," he said. "Six months! What an article for the wall newspaper. Christ! Six months for a few yards of copper wire. How many yards?"

"Four or five," said Comrade Bodi.

"Goddam fool!" said the foreman. "He gets himself six months for five yards of copper wire. No appeal?"

"No appeal."

The foreman looked out of the window. Outside, men were pushing along a wheelbarrow full of scrap. "Nothing will stop them," he muttered. "What a fool. What did he want the copper wire for?"

"To hang out his washing," Bodi said. "Copper doesn't leave rust marks on the washing."

The next day they arrested two of the men who had stolen the leather—a lathe operator of about forty and his accomplice, an old man who worked in the factory stockroom. They had been cutting the straps and hiding them under their coats. The Party organization called a meeting in the main workshop. The manager and Party secretary were there. Three or four hundred men gathered around a big drawing table in the middle of the workshop.

The two culprits stood on the table. The lathe operator, motionless, his face chalk-white, arms dangling, looked down at the sheet of rusty tin plate that covered the table. Beside him the old man stood gawking at the silent crowd. Now and again he smiled: he did not understand what had happened to him. He wore a canary-coloured beret which he kept pushing back and forth on his bald head. He seemed tired from working all night. He shifted his weight to each foot in turn, moving his old lined face to right and left, as if begging for help. Above his head the factory loudspeaker bellowed happy marching tunes.

Comrade Bodi's speech only took a few minutes. The sullen-faced workers listened without moving. When Bodi paused between his slowly spoken sentences, they could hear the scraping of the old man's iron heels on the metal table top. Other workmen arrived from near-by shops, and the crowd around the table grew. Above the table the arm of a crane had stopped in mid-transit. Five or six men stood in the idle bucket, just above the two thieves. The lathe operator stood motionless; sweat ran down his face. The old man continued to rock from one foot to the other, smiling emptily.

Just before the end of the meeting the canary-yellow beret slipped from the old man's head and fell to the floor. An old workman bent down to pick it up and put it on the table. In his confusion the old man rolled it up and stuffed it in his pocket. He left his hand there, and as the meeting ended one might have thought he was listening to Comrade Bodi's speech, smiling jauntily, not caring at all. The men standing near the table saw that he had wet his pants.

Before the morning shift ended, the word went around that the lathe operator had committed suicide. He had hanged himself in the washroom. He had made a noose of brass wire, climbed on a toilet seat. Then, with his head in the noose, he had stepped off into space. When they found him, his body was already cold.

"Well, what did you say at the meeting?" Mrs. Bodi asked when he got home that night.

Comrade Bodi was stretched out on the couch, his head hanging over the edge. He had his usual migraine but seemed calm. The large room was lit only by a little lamp with a pink shade on the bedside table.

"What could I say?"

The pale little woman paced up and down the room, wringing her hands. "My God, my god! The Lord will punish us," she wailed. "They'll all say it's your fault. What did you say?"

"I made a speech," said Bodi.

"Saying what?"

"What I had to say."

The little pale woman went on wringing her hands and wept.

"Don't get upset," said Bodi.

"What?"

"Don't get upset. Sit down. You make me dizzy."

She sat down near him and put a cold, bony hand on his forehead.

"What did you say?"

"I said what I had to say."

"The Lord will punish us. Why did it have to be you?"

"The manager picked me."

"But why did it have to be you?"

Bodi did not answer.

"God will punish us. Why did it have to be you?"

The man tilted his head still farther back, just above the floor which glowed under the red light of the lamp. "I'm a member of the council for discipline," he said, looking at the pallid face of his wife. "It was up to me to speak. I couldn't get out of it."

"What did you say?"

"Stop moving around like that," said Bodi. "You make me dizzy. Sit down on the couch."

The woman sat down again on the couch, at her husband's feet. "The good Lord will punish us," she said, "It was no job for you. You're too good. You'll make yourself ill. How did you speak?"

"With great care," said Bodi, looking up at his wife's face. "I said what I could in his favour."

"What?"

"That he was a first-class skilled worker."

"God will punish us," the woman repeated. "What else did you say?"

"I said that he had worked in the factory for fourteen years. I said that he never missed a single day, that he was a good timekeeper, dependable in his work."

"God will punish us anyway," she said. "What else did you say?"

The man held his head between his hands. "I said that he had been a Party member since 1945, that he had fulfilled all the tasks that the Party set him, but that for some time he had done his political work grudgingly. I said that Communists must set an example . . . that they must always be first . . ."

"Yes," said the woman. "You would say that."

". . . that they must set an example in production and also in discipline."

"Naturally," said the woman. "You said that."

Comrade Bodi looked at his wife's face. It was red in the lamplight. "That's what I said. And I said that when a Communist harms the State and does not respect Socialist property, he is twice a criminal and has no place alongside honest workers."

"God will punish us," said the woman. "He stole because he wasn't earning enough."

Slowly the man lifted his head onto the couch. "That's what they all say."

"Poor man! Look at your own shoes," said his wife. "When will you have the money to buy yourself another pair?"

Comrade Bodi did not look at his shoes. He stared at his wife's face which had aged so much in recent years. Their godchild, who was married and lived in Miskolc, had hardly recognized her when she visited Budapest last winter.

"Go to bed," he said. "I'll sleep on the couch. Turn out the light."

"Did anyone else speak?"

"Yes."

"How many?"

"Two."

"What did they say?"

"They didn't say anything," muttered Bodi. "Go to bed. Put out the light. It was all decided in advance. None of the workers spoke."

"Because they all steal," said the woman. "Poor men. We are poor people, too. When will the poor have a little peace?"

Three days after the suicide, at lunchtime, Comrade Bodi walked down the narrow alley between the metal shop and the red brick wall. He stretched himself out at the base of the wall, his head resting on a brick. He had a headache. A strong wind blew. From time to time a cloud of dust and litter rose and, when the lull in the wind came, fell back to the ground like a veil. The sun went in and out behind the swift clouds. Comrade Bodi stretched out for a moment, then got up, dusted his trousers and went toward the shop. At the end of the alley he saw a man with his back turned toward him, carrying a bulky package under his arm. When the man saw Bodi, he began to run. Bodi continued slowly on his way.

The man turned back. "All right, Bodi!" he said. "You bastard, tell them."

Bodi walked on.

"You saw me, you bastard," the man shouted. "Tell them. Do you think it matters? I'm not afraid to die."

"I won't denounce you," said Bodi.

"You're lying, you louse. I know your kind. I won't run away from you. Come on. Go to the police. Here's the proof for the bastards."

"Get the hell out of here," said Bodi.

The next day Comrade Bodi did not go to the factory. He spent the whole day at home. He fixed the leaky kitchen faucet;

he fixed the washer and packed it with caulking; then he went to see about some plumbing fixtures. He knew the owner of a neighbourhood workshop. He worked until late in the afternoon. Then he fixed the kitchen table and polished the stove. The next day he bought two cans of white paint and painted all the kitchen furniture. He put two coats on the garbage can because the first was rough. He stayed home a week, until the end of the month.

Arriving early, he left Karoly Brock Street, which led to the main gate of the factory, turned into the first side street, and a few minutes later came out onto the bank of the Danube. He still had half an hour before him until the night shift.

The spring sunshine was warm and clear. The light was like crystal over the wide river. On the far bank—Pest—the long row of dust-coloured warehouses was framed by sky, shimmering in the crystal air. Behind them smokestacks rose black, as far as the horizon, in a sky empty of birds. The Danube flowed silently. No ripple disturbed its surface. If it had not been for the sharp stench of ammonia from the factories and the piles of garbage scattered on the sand, he would have stretched out on the ground at the water's edge.

The red brick wall glowed in the sun. In an angle of the wall, well beyond the stockroom, Bodi saw a piece of leather. He walked on his way. A pleasant breeze blew in from the river. Every now and then it drove away the stink from across the brick wall.

"Hello," said the foreman. "Are you better?"

"All right."

"Flu?"

"That's it."

The foreman rummaged around in his desk. "Me too—every year around this time."

The foreman stood up, pushed his steel-rimmed glasses down onto his nose, and went toward the door. He gave Bodi a pat on the back.

"Don't worry, Bodi," he said. "All right?"

"Of course," said Bodi.

"And the wife?"

"Not too bad."

"That's good," said the foreman. He left the cubicle.

A young girl came into the dimly lit place with a little dance step, laughing. She had a face as fresh as the peonies she had been picking that very morning in her garden at Budafok before setting off for the factory.

Comrade Bodi stared vacantly at her for a moment, then, without knowing, sighed and sat down again behind his desk.

In the evening his wife set the table in front of the open window. The window looked out onto the island where the shipyards lay.

"Do you like it?" she asked.

Comrade Bodi liked noodles and cabbage. "Good."

The woman poured out a glass of water for him and cut a piece of bread.

"A headache?"

"No."

"No pain during the day either?"

Bodi thought for a moment. "No. None."

"It makes me laugh," said the woman a little later. "You always have to have a piece of bread with your noodles and cabbage. For eighteen years. You eat bread with everything—soup, vegetables, noodles, even cake."

The man looked at his wife's face, waiting to see what she would say next.

"You told me eighteen years ago, when I gave you your first meal. 'Listen,' you said, 'I'm an eater of bread. I even eat it with noodles. Bread always on the table, always a piece beside my plate.'"

Comrade Bodi continued to look at his wife.

"For eighteen years now I've been cutting bread for you."

Bodi nodded his head. "That's true."

"Of course, it's true," said the woman, laughing. "Eighteen years now. But you don't eat what I cut."

Comrade Bodi looked at the piece of bread lying untouched beside his plate. At his side his wife was laughing so much that her thin, faded face was suddenly filled with a youth that effaced its lines.

"For years now. You sit down to the table, you look to see if there's bread by your plate, then you go after the noodles with a spoon. The bread, that stays where it is."

"It's true."

The woman laughed again. "You're getting old, Bodi."

"I must be," admitted the man.

"You're no longer an eater of bread."

The woman looked out of the window at the Danube, which shone with a dark brilliance.

"You didn't have a headache yesterday, either. Did you? You didn't lie on the couch, and you didn't ask me for medicine."

"Didn't I?"

"No. It must be at least four or five days since you asked for medicine. Unless you bought some yourself."

Staring in front of him, he shook his head. "No, I didn't buy any," he said. "Four or five days?"

"Thank God!" said the woman with a sigh. "Thank God. May the Lord be praised! Perhaps you won't need any tomorrow either."

"Maybe," said Bodi.

He grew suddenly gloomy, stood up and went to the window.

"Maybe," he repeated, morosely, as if to himself.

# LOVE

*Translated by Ilona Duczyńska*

# LOVE

The cell-door opened and the guard tossed something in.

"Grab it," he said.

A sack on which a number was painted fell to the floor in front of the prisoner. B. stood up, took a deep breath and stared at the guard.

"Your stuff," said the guard. "Put it on. They're going to shave you."

In the sack were the clothes and shoes he had taken off seven years ago. The clothes were creased and limp, and the shoes mouldy. He smoothed out the shirt which was also mouldy. When he had dressed, the prison barber came in and shaved him.

An hour later they took him to the small office of the prison. Some eight or ten prisoners were standing around in the corridor all wearing their own clothes, but they called him in first—almost as soon as he reached the office door.

A sergeant sat at the desk, another stood beside him, and a captain paced slowly up and down the small room.

"Come 'ere," said the sergeant at the desk. "Name?"....
...."Mother's name?"......... "Destination?".......

"I don't know," said B.

"What d'yer mean?" asked the sergeant. "Don't yer know your destination?"

"No," said B. "I don't know where they'll take me."

The sergeant made a wry face. "They ain't takin' yer nowhere," he said. "You can go home to the old lady for dinner, and tonight you can have a piece in bed. Get it?"

The prisoner did not answer.

"Destination?"

"No. 17, Szilfa Street."

"Which district in Budapest?"

"Second," said B. "Why are they letting me out?"

"D'yer understand," growled the sergeant. "They're letting yer out. Period! Aren't yer glad to get out of this place?"

His personal possessions were brought in from the next room, a cheap wrist-watch, a fountain pen, and a worn greenish-black wallet that had been his father's. The wallet was empty.

"Sign here," said the sergeant.

It was a receipt for the wrist-watch, the pen and the wallet.

"This one too."

This was another receipt for a hundred and forty-six forints in wages. They counted the money for him on the table.

"Put it away," said the sergeant.

B. took out his wallet and stuffed in the paper money and the change. A musty smell clung to the wallet as well. The last thing he was handed was his letter of discharge. The dotted line marked "reason for arrest" was left blank.

He stood around in the corridor for about an hour. Then they escorted him, together with three other prisoners, to the main gate. Just before they reached the gate a sergeant came running out and stopped them. He picked out one of the four and marched him back to prison, between two guards with tommy guns. The man's newly shaven face turned a sudden yellow. His eyes became glassy.

The three went on to the gate.

"There's the tram, get going," said the guard to B. when he had searched him and returned his letter of discharge.

B. stood there, staring at the ground.

"What are you waiting for?" asked the guard.

B. was still standing, surveying the ground at his feet.

"Get the hell out," said the guard. "What are you hanging around for?"

"I'm going," said B. "You mean I can go?"

The sentry did not answer. B. pocketed his letter of discharge and walked through the gate. After a few steps he wanted to look back, but he checked himself and went on. He listened, but there were no steps behind him. If I make it to the tram, he thought, and no one grabs my shoulder or calls out my name from behind, then, presumably, I'm a free man. Or am I?

When he reached the tram stop, he turned suddenly: nobody was following him. He poked around in his pocket for a handkerchief to wipe the sweat off his forehead, but couldn't find one. He boarded the tram that came screeching along. A prison guard with a pock-marked face was getting off the second car and, in passing B. on the first car, his small piggy eyes looked him up and down. B. did not salute. The tram started.

At that moment—from that split second onward when he did not salute the guard and the tram started—just then, the world broke into sound. Much as in the cinema, when something had gone wrong with the projector and the film had been running silent for a time and, suddenly, right in the middle of a sentence or a word, the sound blasts out of the gaping mouth of the actor. Then the theatre, a deaf-mute space, in which the very public seemed deprived of its third dimension, on an instant impulse is rocked to the rafters with vibrant song, music and dialogue. All about him the colours started exploding. The tram coming from the opposite direction was yellower than any yellow B. had ever seen, and it raced by at such speed past a low, shimmering grey house, that B. thought it would never get under control again. Across the street, two horses, red as poppies, galloped in front of an empty cart. The enchantment of its rattle made the fairy clouds dance in a mackerel sky. A tiny garden, bottle-green, with two sparking glass globes and an open kitchen window undulated past. Millions of people milled about the pavements, all in civilian clothes, no two of them alike and each one lovelier than the other. Many were amazingly small, only knee-high, and some had to be carried. And the women!

Since B. felt that his eyes were swimming, he went inside the tram. The woman conductor's voice was sonorous and very tender. B. bought a ticket and sat down on the first seat at the end of the car. He shut off his senses. If they remained open, he would lose all control. At one moment he saw out of his window on the pavement opposite by the brewery gate, a man caressing the cheek of a young woman. He felt again in his trouser pocket for a handkerchief, but there just wasn't one to wipe the fresh beads of sweat from his forehead. A worker sat down on the empty seat opposite, with a half-dozen bottles of beer in his open brief case.

The conductor laughed.

"Won't it be a bit too much?"

"I'm a married man, sister," said the worker. "My wife likes to watch her old man have a few."

The conductor laughed.

"Just watch?"

"Sure."

"Is it dark beer?"

"Right."

"But light beer is nicer."

"But my wife likes dark to look at."

Again the conductor laughed.

"Why don't you leave me a bottle?"

"Dark?"

"All right, dark."

"What for?"

"I'd take it home for my husband."

"What good is dark to him if he likes 'em fair?"

The conductor laughed. They came to a stop. B. got off and hailed a taxi. The taxi-driver clanked down the tin flag.

"Where to, please?" he said after a while, since his fare said nothing.

"To Buda," said B.

The taxi-driver turned and eyed his passenger.

"By which bridge?"

B. looked straight ahead. Which bridge indeed.

"You a stranger here?" asked the taxi-driver.

"By the Margit Bridge," said B.

The cab started. B. sat erect, not leaning back. The sunlit street's smell of dust and petrol, the clanging bells of the streetcars rushed through the open cab windows. The sun blazed down freely on both pavements and the shadows of the pedestrians, streaking by their feet, seemed to double the volume of traffic. The awnings of a sweet shop had orange stripes which shed russet light on a young woman who sat smoking. Further on at the corner, a small chestnut tree was budding, gathering underneath it a minute patch of lacy, exhilarating shade.

"If you could stop for some cigarettes somewhere . . .' said B. to the cab-driver.

They stopped at the third door. B. looked out of the window: they were directly opposite the open door of a small shop with bundles of red radishes, mounds of green lettuce and red apples in a heap. Beside the shop was the narrow doorway of a tobacconist's.

"I'll get 'em for you," the cab-driver said, turning around. "What brand?"

B. was looking at the radishes. His hands trembled.

"Would it be Kossuths?"

"Yes," said B. "And a box of matches."

The taxi-driver got out. "Don't bother," he said, "we'll put it on the fare. One packet?"

"Yes, please," said B.

The driver returned. "Won't you have one now? My brother-in-law was also in for two years. First thing he did was pick up some cigarettes. Smoked two Kossuths, one after the other, before he went home."

"Can you tell?" asked B. after a while.

"Well, maybe a little," said the driver. "My brother-in-law also had such a sick-lookin' colour. Of course, you migh come from the hospital, but they don't crease your clothes like that. How long y'been in?"

"Seven years," said B.

The driver whistled. "Political?"

"Yes," said B. "A year and a half in the condemned cell."

"And now they let y'out?"

"Looks like it," said B. "Does it show a lot?"

The driver shrugged up both shoulders and let them fall again. "Seven years!" he repeated. "No wonder."

B. got out of the taxi at the funicular railway station, and walked the rest of the way. He wanted to get used to moving about easily, before he met his wife. The cab-driver refused to accept a tip.

"You'll need your money, comrade," he said. "Don't spend it on anything except your health! Get yourself some meat every day, and half a bottle of good wine. That'll put you on your feet in no time."

"Good-bye," said B.

Sideways across the street he saw a narrow mirror in the window of a clothes shop. He stood about in front of it for a while, then he continued on his way. Since the Pasarét Road was full of people, he took a footpath up the hillside, past a tennis-court, to the Hermann Otto Road. But there was too much open space all round him here, with empty lots facing the range of hills opposite. He grew dizzy and sat down on the grass. His wife wasn't expecting him anyway, he thought, so he had time to sit on the grass for half an hour. Facing him was a fence, and behind it stood an apple tree in full bloom. B. looked at it for a while, then went over to the fence. The waxy, shining white flowers were so thick on the boughs that looking up from below into the snow-white dome, one could hardly see the stark blue plane of the vibrant sky. Each flower held at the centre of its large round petals a tinge of pink—a tender touch of colour for its bridal splendour. So many bees buzzed in and out of the petals, that the tree seemed to have a veil over it blowing in the wind. B. stood listening to the tree. He found two boughs through which he could look into the sky, while far away a downy cloud looked like yet another apple tree in bloom. He gazed at the two, through the attainable to the unattainable, till he blacked out.

He had forgotten to wind his wrist-watch and didn't know how much time had passed since he had left the taxi, so he turned and started for home. After a few steps, he went behind a bush and vomited; he felt relieved. After another half-hour's walk through narrow sunlit lanes that criss-crossed a hillside of fruit trees in bloom, he arrived at the house. They lived on the first floor. In the garden, to the right and left of the front door, stood two white lilac bushes. He went up the front stairs.

No one answered the bell. There was no name-plate on the door. He went downstairs to the caretaker's flat and knocked at the door.

"Good morning," he said to the woman who opened the door. She, too, looked thinner and had aged.

"Are you looking for anyone?"

"I am B.," said B. "Is my wife still living here?"

"My God!" said the woman.

B. looked upon the floor. "Is my wife still living here?"

"My God!" said the woman again. "So you've come home?"

"Yes, home," said B. "Is my wife still living here?"

The woman let go of the knob and leaned over against the doorpost. "You've come home," she repeated. "My God! Of course she's living here. And didn't she know that you were coming home, either? My God! Yes of course she lives here."

"My son too?" asked B.

The woman responded. "He's fine," she said. "He's in fine shape, strong and healthy. Good God," B. said nothing.

"But come right in," said the woman, her voice shaky. "Come right in! I knew you were innocent. I knew you'd come home some day."

"But they didn't open the door," said B. "I rang three times."

"Do come in," said the woman again. "There's no one home. The other people are also away."

B. said nothing. He looked upon the floor.

"Your wife is at work, and Gyurika is at school," said the woman. "Won't you come in? They'll be home in the afternoon."

"Are there others in the flat?" asked B.

"Very decent people," said the woman. "Your wife gets along very well with them. Good God, so you did come home!"

B. said nothing.

"I've got the keys to the flat," said the woman after a while, "perhaps you'd like to go upstairs and rest a little before your wife gets home."

On the wall two keys were hanging on a nail. The woman took one and shut the door behind her.

"Perhaps you'd like to go upstairs and rest," she said.

B. glanced down at his feet. "Are you coming, too?" he asked.

"Of course," said the woman, "I'll show you in which room your wife lives."

"In which room does she live?" asked B.

"Well, you know, the other people are four all together," said the woman. "They have the two rooms. Your wife moved into the maid's room with Gyurika. But they share the kitchen and bathroom."

B. did not answer.

"Shall we go on up," asked the woman, "or would you rather wait here with us, till they come home? Just come in and stretch out on the sofa till they come home."

"They share the kitchen and bathroom?" asked B.

"Yes, that's right, they share them," said the woman.

B. raised his head and looked right at the woman. "Then I'm allowed to have a bath?"

"Naturally," said the woman, smiling and putting her hand on B.'s elbow convincingly, "of course you can have a bath, why shouldn't you? It's your flat, isn't it, and as I said, the kitchen and bathroom are shared. I'd be glad to make up a fire for you to warm the water, since we have a little of the wood left over from the winter in the cellar, but for all I know the others keep the bathroom locked in the day-time."

B. said nothing. He glanced down again.

"Shall we go upstairs, then, or would you rather stop in at our place?" asked the woman. "Do come to our place, I'll be in the kitchen and won't disturb you at all. You can lie down on the sofa and maybe even have a nap."

"Thanks," said B., "but I'd rather go upstairs."

The maid's room was tiny and faced northwards, as maids' rooms usually do. The window looked out on an ornamental tree and to the left you could see a dark hilltop covered with pines. The foliage in front of the window made the room seem dark green. As soon as he was alone and his breathing had quietened down, he recognized the fragrance of his wife. He sat down near the window and took a deep breath. In the tiny room there were, all told, a worn white cupboard, an iron bedstead, a table, and a chair; to get to the bed you had

to push the chair out of the way. He did not lie down on the
bed. He just sat and breathed. The table was piled with many
things, books, clothing, toys. There was also a small hand-
mirror. He looked into it; it showed what the one in the shop
window had shown. He put it back on the table, facing down-
wards. He didn't disturb his wife's things on the table. A
child's rubber ball with red dots rested on the ash-tray. His
wife's fragrance lingered over the table too.

He had hardly sat down when the caretaker's wife came in
with a large jug of milky coffee and two thick slices of white
bread. He ate it as soon as he was alone. Soon afterwards, the
ground-floor tenant's wife rang the bell. She also brought
coffee, bread and butter, sausage and a red apple like the ones
he had seen in the small shop in the street. She put the tray
on the table. His eyes were moist and she left after a few
minutes. When B. was alone, he ate it. He still hadn't wound
his wrist-watch and didn't know how long he'd been sitting
near the window. The window looked out on the back
garden where there was no one. The tree had leaves with
white borders which rustled lightly in the wind, and the
afternoon light glowed on the white-washed walls of the tiny
room.

When he had breathed in so much of his wife's fragrance that
he didn't notice it any more, he went down into the street near
the garden gate. Soon afterwards his wife turned the corner
with four or five little boys around her. She came towards
the gate, her steps suddenly slackening. She even stopped
short for a second, then ran towards him. B. also started
running without knowing it. As they neared each other the
woman slowed up, as if uncertain, but soon ran forward. B.
recognized the long-sleeved grey woollen pullover she was

wearing, which he had bought for her in a shop down town just before his arrest. His wife was a wonderful blend of air and flesh, unseen and unheard of before; unique. She surpassed everything he had treasured about her for seven years in prison.

When they separated from each other's arms, B. leaned against the fence. A few paces behind his wife stood four or five little boys, with curious, if somewhat perturbed, faces. They were about six or seven years old. There weren't five, but really only four. Leaning against the fence, B. looked at them, one by one.

"Which one is mine?" he asked.

At this point she began to cry.

"Let's go upstairs," she said, crying.

B. put his arms round her shoulders.

"Don't cry."

"Let's go upstairs," she said, sobbing openly.

"Don't cry," said B. "Which one is mine?"

The woman swung open the garden gate and went running between the two lilac bushes to the house. She disappeared in the entrance. She was still as slim as when they had parted and she ran with the same long, elastic strides as once, when she was a girl she had run away from a cow, with uncontrolled fear in her legs. But when B. reached her upstairs in front of the door to the flat she had calmed down; only her girlish breasts heaved under her grey sweater. She was no longer crying, but her eyelids were still moist beneath the tears she had wiped away.

"My dearest," she whispered, "my dearest."

When she whispered, each word could almost be taken in one's mouth as it hung in the air.

"Let's go in," said B.

"There are other people living in the flat too now."

"I know," said B., "Let's go in."

"Have you been inside yet?"

"I have," said B. "Which is my son?"

Once inside, the woman knelt on the floor and put her head in his lap and cried. White threads glistened in her light brown hair with an alien lustre. "My darling, I waited for you. My darling."

B. stroked her head. "Was it hard?"

"My darling," whispered the woman.

B. kept stroking her hair. "Did I grow very old?"

The woman clasped his knees and drew him close. "You are the same as when you left, for me."

"Did I grow very old?" asked B.

"I'll love you always, as long as I live," whispered the woman.

"Do you love me?" asked B.

The woman's back trembled. She wept openly. B. took his hand from her head. "Can you get used to me?" he asked. "Will you ever get used to me again?"

"I've never loved anyone else," she said. "I love you."

"Did you wait for me?"

"I was with you every day," said the woman. "There wasn't a day that I didn't think of you. I knew you would come back. But if you hadn't, I would have died alone. Your son was you all over again."

"Do you love me?" asked B.

"I've never loved anyone else," she said "I'd love you, no matter how you've changed."

"I've changed," said B. "I've grown old."

The woman wept, she pressed B.'s foot close to her. B. stroked her hair again.

"Can we still have a child?" she asked.

"Perhaps," said the man, "if you love me. Please get up."

The woman got up.

"Shall I call him?"

"Not yet," said B. "Let me stay a while longer with you. He's still a stranger. Did he stay in the garden?"

"I'll go downstairs to him," said the woman. "I'll tell him to wait."

When she returned, B. was standing at the window, with his back to the room. His back was narrow and awry. He did not turn. The woman stood in the doorway for a moment. "I told him to pick some flowers for his father," she said, a little hoarse with emotion. "The lilacs are in bloom over on the next allotment, and he should pick a big bunch for his father."

"Do you love me?" asked B.

The woman ran up to him, clasped his shoulders and nestled in close. "My only one," she said.

"Can you get used to me?" asked B.

"I've never loved anyone else," said the woman. "I was with you night and day. Every day I talked to your son about you."

B. turned around, he embraced the woman and looked closely at her face. In the rays of sunset that fell through the window, he saw with some relief that she, too, had aged, though she was more beautiful than the image he had recalled every day for seven years. Her eyes were closed, her mouth partly open and her hot breath touched B.'s cheeks. Thick eyelashes covered the pale skin under her moist eyes. She was meekness itself. B. kissed her eyes, then tenderly moved her away from himself.

"Love our boy, too," she said, with her eyes still closed.

"Yes," said B. "I'll get to know him and love him."

"He's your son!"

"And yours," said B.

The woman clung to his neck. "I'll wash you," she said.

"Good."

He stripped. She made the bed, laying her husband's naked body on the sheet. She brought warm water in a tin pan, soap and two towels. She folded one, dipped it in the water and put soap on it. She washed the whole body down to his feet. Twice she changed the water. B.'s hand still twitched now and then, but his face was at peace.

"Can you get used to me?" he asked.

"My darling," said the woman.

"Will you sleep with me tonight?"

"Yes," she said.

"Where does the boy sleep?"

"I'll make a bed for him on the floor," said the woman. "He sleeps soundly."

"Will you stay with me all night?"

"Yes," said the woman, "every night as long as we live."